TIDINGS OF TULIPS

Tidings of Tulips

YULE TIDINGS

Lukas Allen

Lukas Allen

Contents

For the weary traveler who stumbled onto this book by accident

1

Yule

"Just drop it, Jake! We don't need it!" I yelled at him. He was carrying a giant armful of booze, dropping bottles here and there which shattered on the street as he ran to us. The mob nearly caught up with him, but I pulled him into the back just in time, and Dina raced us off in the van. He spilled the booze bottles all over the floor of the van, and grinned wide. "You idiot... I told you I wanted to try the sober life!" I said.

"Yeah, yeah, Yule... But that was only because we ran out of booze. I saw you diluting those last drops of whiskey over and over again, tryin' to get any bit of alcohol." Jake said.

I frowned at him, but he just grinned at me, happiness in his three eyes... and I couldn't stop myself from grinning too, and then laughing.

And then kissing him, as we cuddled in the back of the van, littered in treasure, tons of booze.

We soon got back to our hidden hideout, a giant abandoned camp-site, an old natural park right next to a *huge* waterfall... Niagara Falls.

Dina helped me take out the loot we got, booze, food, and supplies, and she said, "That was an alright grocery trip... Although I sure wish the place wasn't covered in cannibals."

"Eh. It happens. Everything sure is crazy right now." I said.

"I think we were only living in a little bubble before... and then pop, we were thrown back into the natural order of things." Dina said.

Jake stacked the booze next to the fire, showing Lux, who was a golem, Cass, who had robotic limbs, and Zax, the alcohol. They cheered at him, even though Lux didn't need to drink, and Cass soon frowned. The cat and the dog laid peacefully by the fire against each other.

We laughed and hollered as we opened up the first bottle of booze and passed it around, swigging from it.

I put the bottle to my lips, and tasted the ambrosial nectar of good moonshine. Those cannibals sure knew what they were doing when it came to distilling.

We laughed and joked with each other, as I sat on Jake's lap. I sighed in contentment with his arms around me, and listened to the distant waterfall...

But... I heard something else as well. I heard... No... That couldn't be... Was it the sound of a flute?

I told everyone to be quiet for a second.

The flute music came closer and closer, giving us goosebumps.

I got up off of Jake, and ran to the sound of that music.

There was a man walking under the full moon, a man clothed in black, passing through the trees in complete silence, besides the sound of the beautiful music he was playing.

I wanted to remain quiet and listen to that music some more, but he was walking away from me, so I called out, "Lucius!'

He stopped playing, and the crickets resumed their song, the night birds hooted, and Lucius turned to me, surprised.

I ran up to him and hugged him. "Yule?" he said.

"Yeah, you damn man! I thought I'd never see you again!" I said, smiling at his bearded face and long hair. Hair that wasn't black like mine anymore... no, it was blonde. I ran a hand through his blonde hair and smiled in delight at him.

The others found us, and were just as surprised as me. They went up to him, hugging and cheering for him.

We had our Dark Piper back.

Jake put an arm around my shoulder, and I put an arm around Jake's waist, and he said, "Holy fuckin shit. We missed you, man. Next time you don't just- don't just- Fuckin' leave a note or somethin', for Christ's sake!"

Lucius looked at us, and said, "I thought it would be wiser to leave without all the hassle of goodbyes. I didn't want you all to chain me down or something, thinking I was going to meet my end out here."

Cass said, "Why did you leave? I prayed for you every day, and I'm glad God heard my prayers."

"I needed to be with nature. Life is- It's just awesome. I- I have something for you, Yule." Lucius said, and took something out of his coat, that was gently wrapped in cloth... and I gasped.

It was a flower that wasn't black. It was the reddest tulip I had ever seen.

2

Lucius

Dina was talking to the black and grey cat, who only seemed to mewl up at her.

Yule stared at the flower, that was as red as her naturally red albino eyes, as red as the hoodie that she was wearing. She had long black hair rolling down to her neck. I talked with the rest of my- my friends. The people that I left for so long... The people that I loved.

I said, "So... I see you guys found color, too."

Cass, the woman with robotic arms and legs, showed off her shirt for me, which was a rainbow colored tie dye shirt. "We looted a clothing store that had been sealed!" she said, "Nothing in it turned black, and still they haven't turned black yet!"

"The pollution is lifting, strangely. Organic fiber isn't turning black anymore. You guys watch the sun set too now?" I said.

Cass nodded to me, and said, "It is truly the majesty of God. I believe that it is a sign that He is coming back to this world, reclaiming it one step at a time."

"The darkness is lifting, and the light shines again. Those fucking black clouds aren't as thick, anyway." I said.

Jake, a guy with three eyes, gave me some booze that they all had, and said, "We were going to drink before you left, right? We were going to have a little contest... Well, let's see how drunk we can get you now! This is your homecomin' party, dude!"

I smiled and drank. Jake was usually rather pissy in the morning because of hangovers, every morning, but it was great to drink with him during the evenings. His scars that he had all over his body, from when he used to cut himself, seemed to be faded in the light of the campfire.

Lux, the robot, said, "I could've better equipped you before you began traversing all across creation."

I said, "Nah, no thanks. I really just needed what I already had."

"Really? A toothbrush, half a can of beans, and a machete?" Lux said.

"And my flute." I said.

"I was just beginning to rely on your music always being here, but then it was gone. It was quiet for a while, after you left." Zax said.

Dina turned from her conversation with the cat, and said, "I know you found something cool out there. How about you tell us about it?"

They all agreed. Yule said, "Please tell me where you found this." raising her flower. I looked at the dog, Doug, a black, scarred pitbull with one eye, watching the forest around us. I could tell he wanted to go back out there too, as I did.

But I turned back to my friends, smiled, and told them about my adventures.

I told them of the green trees, huge as skyscrapers, I told them of the animals, coming back to the world again, growing colorful fur and feathers that weren't only black, bears, moose, eagles, cardinals, elk and mountain lions, I told them of the stars in the less clouded sky of the magnificent, quiet wilderness. And I told them about my struggles too.

I was always hungry, but soon the constant grumbling of my stomach became natural and comfortable. I was cold, I was wet, and I was lost until I figured out I could find my way from the natural occurrences of the world, like the stars, the wind, the sun and even the moss on the trees. And I was very lonely...

Until I learned that nature is always beside you. You are nature, and you will never be lonely with her. She is the constant companion, she is our heartbeat, our breath, and with her I soon found out I had all the love I could ever want.

I still looked at Yule longingly however…

But I told her about the time I took shelter in a cave one time. I wandered inside, exploring, and found a deeper cavern with an opening in the ceiling with a hot spring… with flowers of all hues blooming for only me.

I bathed in that pool, and the blackness in my hair left, it washed away, and my natural color came out. I never knew I had blonde hair.

And I said, "I picked only that flower, because it reminded me of you, Yule."

She blushed red, and said, "I want to see this magical place of yours."

"I can take you to it. It's not far. I can show you all how to remove the pollution from your bodies." I said.

"I would love that." she said, and sat beside me, "We don't have to chain you down to keep you from leaving, do we?" she said.

I laughed, and said, "No, I'll stay here for the night. I learned of great roots and berries to eat out there, through very difficult trial and error, and I can cook you all something nice tomorrow."

"Oooh. Nice. Ok, well, I'm going to bed. You need somewhere to sleep?" Yule said.

"I'm just going to sleep out here, by the fire, on the ground, if that's ok." I said.

"Ok. Well, goodnight, Lucius… Dark Piper." she said, smiled, and kissed me on the cheek.

The rest went to bed, Jake and Yule getting in their own tent, Cass and Dina getting in theirs with the dog and the cat, Zax in a tiny tent just for himself, and Lux going to rest in the van.

I stared at the fire, enjoying the silence, at peace.

But I was still a little jealous of the sound of sex in Yule and Jake's tent.

3

Yule

Jake and I had sex. He loved it when I used my hands...

When I strangled him to near death.

When we were done, his three eyes glazed over, and I let him breathe again. He instantly gasped deeply, and I smiled and kissed him.

I was starting to sleep beside him... His beautiful scarred body...

And I thought of that gorgeous flower.

I got aroused again, so we had another round.

In the morning, I put the flower in my black hair, humming to myself after such a nice night, such a deep rest.

I looked down at Lucius by the remains of the fire. Gosh, he looked like he was sleeping even better than I had, even just on the ground outside. I nudged him awake, and he blinked his eyes open and smiled to me.

We went on a short hike, as I let Jake and the others sleep in. I told Lucius all about us scavenging, looting, and trying to survive off the remnants of civilization. "I could understand how you got tired of it." I said.

"It just wasn't the right way for me anymore. Living out here, it makes me feel ten times better. Hard to believe I grew up in a city, when I look back at myself." Lucius said.

"I rather like the woods. It reminds me of being a kid again." I said.

He showed me a cluster of blackberries, and I helped him pick them. He dug up some roots that he promised were edible and had a unique earthy flavor, and he climbed a tall tree and picked some walnuts. I admired his body up above me. He looked quite muscular now.

We went back to the campsite, and he roasted the nuts, mashed the berries into jam, and ground the roots up with two flat stones he had, and sprinkled them on.

I ate nature's bounty with him, and it was strangely... a very nostalgic tasting meal, like something I had when I was young, in the Black Forest of Germany.

I shared with him our food as well, wrapped up snack cakes, eggs, some sausage...

Doug smelled our sausage first, and started barking in Dina's tent, which woke the rest of them up as well.

We soon were all eating breakfast and saying good morning to each other.

Jake still grumbled in our tent however, and remained in bed.

"It's gonna be gone if you don't get out here soon, Jake!" I yelled at him.

"Fuck off, Yule... My head is poundin', and I swear you broke my throat..." Jake said.

I shrugged, and we soon had finished the food. I left Jake some of the snack cakes for when he'd eventually get up around lunch time.

I asked Zax how he slept, if he was still having that dream.

And Zax grimaced, showing his extra incisor, and said, "I had it again last night. But there's more."

He looked down at the mannacle on his wrist, a demon electricity handcuff, and told us of his dream...

4

Zax

I have it every night. Sometimes twice a night.

And I knew my time would be short.

For the archnemesis of creation had already claimed me, as he had claimed my wife and son.

It started off pleasantly... happily... and once I knew it was, I knew the dream would get worse.

I tried to protect my son, my little baby, holding him in my arms...

As I told Rita to not go outside. She said she just wanted to see the beautiful sunlight.

"Please, no, Rita! Don't go outside!" I said, carrying Paul, as she went to the door.

And she ignored me, and went outside anyway.

When she stepped through the door, there was no light outside.

It was only a dark pit, blackness, silence, and death.

I was hyperventilating, even in a dream, as I had watched her leave. I knew she had already left years ago, dying giving birth.

And I looked down at Paul in my arms.

But he wasn't there. Swaddled in cloth... was nothing.

There had never been a Paul, and there would never be a Paul.

And someone lit a cigarette behind me, and I clenched my fists angrily.

"Get out of my home, Satan." I said, without turning.

He just laughed, that awful, evil laugh.

I was very familiar with it by this point.

"You were my challenge, Zaxazaxar... I was not yours. You thought you imprisoned me... but you only wrapped the chains around yourself." Satan said.

"Get out of my head." I said angrily, turning to the Beast.

"That's it... Get angry. You were always destined for me, you know. Just as your forebears were..." Satan said.

"My ancestors escaped your clutches, over and over. As will I." I said.

"And I'm going to break that cycle, Zaxazaxar. You've already broken it, yourself..." he said.

"Leave me *alone!!*" I roared, and shot fireballs from the machine on my wrist, my mannacle as I now knew it to be.

But Satan was the flame, as the house began to burn in horrible demonic electricity.

All I could smell was the smoke and brimstone, and I knew I would die again in this recurring dream, in horrible agony that felt lifelike.

But I did not die this time.

The flames licked up and down my arms... and they almost felt comforting.

Accepting me as their own.

I screamed out, as the horns ruptured from my head, the claws burst from my hands and feet, giant bat wings erupted from my back and the tail sprouted from my behind.

And I laughed, feeling a horrible, awesome sense of evil in me. All I needed to do was to accept it.

I was Zaxazaxar, and I was a demon.

The albino woman with black hair and star tattoos all over her body, the once angel of Heaven called Yule, said, "And that's the end of it?"

"The end of it is me killing all of you." I said, "I don't feel safe around you all... for all of you. But I don't know how to change my fate alone."

"Nothing is written, yet." Dina said, "Don't go into that pit. I'll be there for you next time."

I looked over to this woman with tattoos of American animals and a lighthouse with a skull on top on her skinny arms. I looked deep into her eyes... and I nodded.

Cass came to my side, held my hand with her robotic hand, and said, "Do you want to pray with me for a while?"

I said, "I don't see the point of it anymore. I'm starting to lose faith."

"It makes you feel better if anything, Zax." Cass said.

"...It does." I said, and I held her cyborg hand and we walked to the falls.

We looked down at that huge waterfall. It was so loud we couldn't even hear our own thoughts. It was sort of like listening to silence, in a way.

And I truly could see, as Cass said, the majesty of God in this beautiful natural landmark.

We held hands, and prayed as hard as we could. I prayed for all of my friends, for my wife, Rita, for-

Paul, my son.

And I broke down crying.

Was I even praying for a real person when I prayed for him?

Cass just hugged me, and we sat down on the bench as I cried on her shoulder.

In the evening I was about to get in my tiny tent for one, but Dina grabbed my hand and said, "C'mon. You look restless. Let's burn off some of that extra energy so you can sleep soundly."

I asked her what she meant, but she just called out to Cass, and Cass took my other hand, and they led me into their tent.

They began undressing as I watched. They were both beautiful women, and I hadn't made any advances on either of them, so I was surprised when they, naked, began taking off my clothes as well.

They kissed each other in front of me, and felt each other with one hand... and me with the other.

And well. Love with two women at the same time... It surely can be magical, especially when love is reciprocated by all parties.

I was falling asleep with them in their tent, Cass's robotic arms around me, me unable to leave her embrace if I wanted to, her breasts pressed against my back... and Dina laying in front of me, with those beautiful eyes...

And her eyes went black.

I fell asleep...

5

Dina

This is a world of dreams. And that's right, I'm talking to you.

This is a fantasy, a fiction, kind of like a mirage.

You will never be able to touch it, but you can still dream of the taste of water in the distance.

My name is Dina, and I am a character in this story.

I turned to Zax, with him and his family in his house, as Rita kept saying she wanted to go and see the sunlight, and Zax begging her not to go outside.

Zax was holding an empty swaddle of cloth, but kept on looking at the cloth like it was his pride and joy.

I told Zax, "Let her go outside."

He looked at me quizzically, but was silent as Rita opened the door and left.

Zax looked down at the cloth, crying, and I said to him, "This Paul never lived, Zax. But there is another Paul who did."

We heard the sound of someone starting a cigarette behind us. Zax-azaxar immediately looked angry, but when he turned to the source of that sound… he dropped the bundle of cloth in shock, and stepped back aways.

And Paul, Zax's ancestor, said as he smoked the cigarette, "Heya, Zax. It's nice to meet you."

"Y-You must be some trick. Just like the rest of this dream." Zaxazaxar said.

Paul came up to Zax, and burst out smiling, "Holy shit! You look just like me! Well, besides that extra incisor in your mouth. I guess I've just got strong genes... At least you don't have wings and a tail like I did though. Must be Maggie's half of the family."

"I don't have wings and a tail... yet. But that time will come soon." Zax said.

Paul frowned, rubbed his chin, and said, "Hmm... I expected this, at some point... My genetic father was a demon, actually. It makes sense that his action that led to my birth would still haunt us..."

"I am *really* a descendent of an actual demon??" Zax said, "But- But- I caught the Devil! I subjugated every demon for a time! You mean I am no better than those I conquered??"

"You are much better than them. You try to change. I didn't get to Heaven because I believed I was damned, I did because I was blessed with free will, and used this power to make right again." Paul said.

"But- But- I am chained to the Devil! Do you not see this device on my wrist?? It is an eternal mark of my eternal damnation!! I have no choice but to go down the road to Hell now..." Zax said.

Paul looked at the manacle on Zax, and said, "It looks like a key, rather than a lock."

"That was its intention, to keep the Devil imprisoned. But he turned it back on me." Zax said.

"Hm. Maybe you should find out what this key opens? Maybe the chains on you can be used to free yourself... and others." Paul said.

"...I don't know... I would have to search everywhere just to figure out a purpose for it... and a purpose for myself..." Zax said.

"That's the fun part of life. Keep at it, Zax. And who's this gorgeous woman over here? She's not your girlfriend, is she? Pleased to meet you, Miss. I'm Paul, also known as Spawn of Sax." Paul said, and shook my hand politely.

I smiled. I was all aflutter... I had wanted to meet Paul since when I first heard his music, his ancient, astounding music.

The dream was then just us three drinking coffee and talking about music. Satan was watching in the shadows... but unlike me, he wasn't also acting in the dream.

So I let Paul and Zax joke and laugh, and wandered further into the dreamworld.

Satan whispered beside me, *"I'm going to get him, you know. I'll get you eventually too-"*

I turned to him, and showed him my true form.

A normal human being. Well, a normal human being who's seen past the veil.

I looked into the Devil's eyes with my eyes that have seen through every barrier of every existence, past the veil and beyond.

I showed him I was not afraid, and that I am stronger than my nightmare.

I took a step towards him, and the Devil stepped back.

The Devil ran from me, as I chased him through the darkness and light of reality and fiction.

I stretched awake. What a pleasant dream...

6

Cass

Dina was getting out of the tent as I woke up, as I was still clutched to Zax.

Zax yawned, and stretched an arm around me.

I smiled as I looked into his eyes. I'm glad that Dina and I could include someone in our love for a change.

Zax and I just stayed together for a while, in comfort in each other's arms.

But I really had to use the bathroom!

I kissed Zax good morning, and went out to do my business.

I hummed along back to the campsite. The sun was so brilliant! What a nice morning.

Yule was showing Lucius our maps, and Lucius was pointing to where he believed his cavern would be.

I looked inside Jake's opened tent, and saw him mumbling to himself laying down, in hungover agony.

I had enough of this! Every morning, he'd do the same thing! Just mumble and groan whenever the sun starts to shine! I was glad for a while, when I sneakily hid all the extra booze we had, but then they go off and find more! My friends needed to see the majesty of life sober for a change.

So I decided to change things right now, and banged pots and pans right beside Jake's head.

He screamed awake, and I yelled, "GOOD MORNING, SLEEPING BEAUTY!! IT'S TIME TO WAKE!! GET UP, GET UP, GET UP!!"

He looked at me frightened for a second, and said, "Wha'?? Are you tryin' to fuckin' kill me??"

I said, "No, but I'm going to if you don't get outside and eat some breakfast with us."

He looked at me warily, but slowly got up, got dressed, and came outside with me.

Yule smiled at him, and said, "Finally, someone got you out of bed."

Jake grumbled, and picked a sausage off of the frying pan over the fire, juggling it for a second as it was searing, and said, "Bed's where we have the most fun anyway, Yule. I'd live there with you if I didn't have to eat and shit."

Yule said, "You make it sound so appealing. Well! Too bad, because we're going with Lucius on a hike today."

He groaned, and chomped on his sausage. At least he was eating something again! All he seemed to consume was alcohol.

I went to Lux, who was busy on the van. I said to him, "Good morning, Lux! I was wondering if you could take a look at my left arm when you're finished."

Lux got out from under the van, and said, "Oh, I'm just taking precautionary measures. I can look at your arm now."

I sat down beside him, as he inspected my robotic arm and asked me what the problem was.

"Well you see… When I twist it this way, my grip gets stuck." I said, twisted my arm, and showed him my hand getting stuck. "It didn't matter last night, because Zax didn't seem to notice… He just thought I really enjoyed feeling his penis in my hand. I can't feel anything with my limbs, and just have to guess some of the time. I was worried I would accidentally rip it off of him, though, or squish it into jam!" I said.

"Hmm... I had the same problem when I used to work the streets as a hooker bot. I did squish some of them into jam, actually, before I quit that life. For you it's actually a problem with your rotator cuff reacting with the attached nerves to your cyborg limbs. I'd take it easy for a while, and use that oil on your wrist as well, so the grip doesn't get stuck for too long. What strenuous activities have you been doing? Don't tell me it's something sexual..." Lux said.

"I've been beating up trees... I wanted to work on my form, and I can't fight these guys, or I may kill them... well, besides Yule. But she gets so serious when she fights, and it's hard to get her to take it easy when she does." I said.

"Hm. You've been doing that left jab repeatedly?" Lux said.

"It was the one thing I wasn't very good at. My left side was always weaker when I boxed, so I wanted to strengthen it." I said.

"I don't see the point of you exercising your limbs when they're made of metal now." Lux said.

"I know... but it's more of a mental activity, rather than a physical one." I said.

"Just relax for a while. Let Dina give you a massage, and only a massage, so you can relax and get well again." Lux said.

I smiled, and thanked him, giving him a huge hug.

7

Lux

That silly cyborg... Beating up trees! Who could ever think of such a thing. I wonder what grudge she had against the poor plant life?

I looked back at the van. It was the only other intricate piece of machinery besides me, and she sure needed a lot of love. It was my pleasure spending time on such a beauty. I feel like she felt the same way towards me, as I could practically feel her purr as I started her up to see if everything was still working well.

My baby seemed to be in tip top form, so I let her rest, and talked with the lifeforms I surrounded myself with. I never expected to go down this road with my new friends before. I truly did hate all beings who had a soul at one point of my existence, and I didn't care if they felt happy or sad, suffering or pleasure, or lived or died. But I can safely say my opinions have changed towards a few of them. They aren't as annoying as they were, I think.

No... What really annoys me is that little, white, digital rabbit who is now infected in my programming.

I had tried to purge myself of it endlessly! But still, it keeps on telling me to check my emails! I deleted every account I had ever owned, but it just keeps on making more of them for me! The internet doesn't even work anymore, since society is collapsing back to the stone age, but I still see a digital white rabbit, reminding me of the annoyances of technology.

Yule could see this little white rabbit as well, since she ate a nanobot to go onto the internet once, and it seems to have remained permanently in her despite the company's promises it wouldn't... but she tries to make the most of our time with our new "friend." She told Clippers the white, digital rabbit to play music for us, and took my hands and danced with me.

The others all looked at us quizzically as we danced to only tunes we could hear... Except Dina, who seemed to sense things even I was unable to. Dina clapped her hands in time to the music, as Yule and I turned and circled with each other.

I spun Yule, lifted her up in my arms, and she knew all the moves correctly and precisely. She truly had grace like none other, maybe learning even more new moves when she worked as a stripper for a time, and I was glad I had brought her back to life.

Oh yes... Did I mention that the woman every man in our camp fawned over was actually once an angel? I had snagged her lost spirit into a body that was exactly alike to the one she had, for rather selfish goals... But, we've grown past that in this new life of ours we all have embarked on. I'm glad that Yule could enjoy her life again, with such kind friends as these. The two other women were the luckiest, because Yule preferred their company the most. I wondered how long this relationship with Jake would last... They both seemed very happy together, when they weren't too drunk.

I was glad I didn't need to drink, when I saw what it did to humans. They think they're on top of the world, the most charismatic, the most beautiful, strongest, and smartest... But the reality hardly holds up to their drunken fantasy.

When people got drunk... all they seemed to really want to do is fuck or fight. It was animalistic, but even the two animals we had showed better manners than them! Jake and Yule screamed at each other sometimes, actually threatening to beat each other to a pulp, sometimes even doing so, especially when the alcohol had run out and withdrawal was starting to kick in. It was quieter when she used to share her tent with Dina and Cass...

And now Lucius was back, playing that constant flute music, so I suppose I had to give up on it being quiet altogether. Lucius was curious to me... What had he found out there in the wilds that seemed to complete him so? Was there something that I was missing as a robot? Something that I would never ever have, no matter how hard I tried?

I still do not believe I have a soul... I brought Yule's soul back to this Earth through laborious experimentation, and I still find the idea of having one myself to be inconceivable, and actually quite preferable. I knew all about demon electricity, harvesting a demon's soul for power, and experimented with Yule's lost soul as well. Yet still, the master of souls, me, had no soul.

But I do not think it was something to do with souls that Lucius found... Perhaps he found something that his soul belonged to.

I still stayed back with the cat as they took their hike.

8

Jake

I tried to smile and enjoy it... Like I did when I heard it in the evening with a thick bottle of scotch...

But that flute music was sure gettin' on my nerves.

And Yule kept on staring at 'im as he played... Stroking that flower behind her ear...

This hike to this magic cavern better be worth it...

We travelled with a few bits o' stuff, Yule with a sack of food and cookin' junk on her back, clanging as she hiked vigorously.

God she had a nice butt, in those pure white pants we looted from that store...

I never had found a woman who so completed me in the bed. It was like- It was like- Like Heaven had finally smiled on me... when she smiled too...

We stopped for a rest, and had a little campfire. Yule finally turned her attention from Lucius as she was talkin' with him all day, and looked at me, as I rolled up my sleeves and chopped firewood. I could tell she was gettin' horny just watching me work, as she smiled with a hand on her chest. The others sat around the campfire in silence, as I brought the wood.

I sighed, staring down at my arms. So many scars...

Yule had told me that wasn't who I was anymore, that I had changed... I was sort of like her project, a giant scarred trainwreck of a man, and she worked her hardest to build something out of the scraps of broken bone and scarred muscle that I was.

And well, she kinda succeeded.

I felt like a gentleman with her, and I tried my hardest to please her in other ways than just in the bed. I looked at my past life in shame... Being an executioner, foolishly thinking I was doing good by ending lives efficiently.

And every scar I had represented a life I had taken while working as an executioner for those demons in that prison.

I had tried to nearly die over and over, for every life that was now gone because of me. The blood spilled from my arteries after I sliced myself, the poison would make my vision blur... But I felt like I needed to do it, I needed to show my penance. I thought I was making things fair.

But Yule showed me how messed up that was. Because even though I *nearly* died a few times... the lives I took *had* died. It was like throwing a penny to a beggar, when you had a hundred bucks in your wallet. He couldn't even buy a meal with that penny, but I could buy 20 meals, and continued my life as well.

Lucius said we would be there in the evening.

I tried to get some alone time with Yule, walking with her aways from the others...

But as I was kissing her in that gentlemanly fashion she liked so much, she didn't kiss me back, and said, "Stop it, Jake. I thought you just wanted to take a walk or something."

"We walked, didn't we?" I said, grinning. She always loved that grin.

She cocked her head to the side, and said, "Well, we can walk back now, too."

I held her hand, preventing her from walking away, and said, "Is something wrong?"

She sighed, and said, "I don't know. I just feel like *washing* for Christ's sake... I'm sweaty from walking all day, probably have a few ticks, and I don't feel like strangling you right now."

I frowned, and said, "But that's how we first met... I thought, y'know, it was nostalgic or somethin'."

She said, "No, Jake. I see that really it's just another form of your messed up penance thing. You think it's alright because it's somebody else doing it... But it's not."

"Well, we don't need to do tha' anymore, then." I said, and took both her hands and looked deep into her red eyes, saying, "Yule... I feel like you complete me. I love you, an' I want to go back to the country with you, maybe have a farm again. We can raise those pigs you like eatin-"

But she sighed, and said, "I don't think that will work."

I opened my three eyes in surprise, as I heard someone playin' a flute.

She continued, "The world is in the worst place it has ever been. I can't continue to just hide from the suffering others are going through. It's- It's my duty to be like an angel on Earth for those people. It's my calling to bring light in the darkness, to save those in Hell's grasp."

"Wha'?? That's suicide, babe. How can you demean me for hurting myself when you want to go and end your life altogether?" I said, "We just need to let things blow over. It'll get better over time."

"I'm sorry, Jake. But you can join me, if you like." she said.

I took my hands from hers, and said, "You like the flute boy, don't you."

"What?? I just told you that you can change the world *with* me!" I said.

"No... I get it. You've been enraptured by his seducing song again. You don't give a shit about the world, you're just trying to give me an excuse so you can make your getaway… You just make me sick." I said angrily.

She looked furious for a second, extremely pissed.

So I said, "Gonna beat the shit outta me again? So what. I'm used to your fightin' style now. Try it, if you like."

She was actually about to throw a punch, and I put my fists up too and grinned. She loved a good fight, and once it was over, we were cuddled up in bed and moaning each other's names.

But she saw that grin, and put down her fist. She calmed down, and said, "Have fun with the pigs, Jake."

And she walked away from me, to that stupid music.

9

Yule

I had furiously grabbed up Lucius in the middle of a song, and forced him to take me on a walk.

I just felt so angry... And if Jake thought I liked "the flute boy" then I'd let him think it ten times over...

But my anger was dispelled immediately, as I gasped at the huge tree under the rising moon that Lucius showed me.

"They get bigger and bigger in the north. I guess they had to grow more to get to any ounce of sunlight that they could out here." Lucius said.

I just put a hand to the tree. It felt like I was touching time itself.

But beneath the tree... was a cave.

And Lucius said, "This is actually where I found the flower, in this exact spot. We can wait until the morning so the others can see it too in the day-"

But I said, "Screw that!! I want to see this mystical garden *now!* Let's go, let's go, let's go!"

Lucius smiled, and led me through the darkness of the cave, taking my hand so I wouldn't lose my way. He seemed to have instincts honed to a razor's edge now, and while I stumbled and tripped in the darkness, Lucius held my hand and prevented me from falling.

We went through the twisty darkness, as I put all my trust into Lucius knowing his way through the cavern.

And then... I saw light around the corner. We walked to it, as I trembled in anticipation, hoping it would be as I imagined it...

And I was not disappointed.

It was a paradise of color, as the moon shone down through the top onto the plant life.

I knelt before the flowers, as a few of the night ones opened their petals and bloomed for no one's eyes but ours.

And I looked at the pool, the pool that Lucius promised he had gotten blonde hair in.

I undressed, and walked into the pool. Lucius sat at the edge and watched me wash myself, cleansing myself of darkness and evil.

I tried to wash my hair, and Lucius told me to submerge in the water.

I held my breath, and submerged myself in the warm water.

And when I resurfaced, Lucius gasped this time.

I felt my long albino white hair. It felt so soft and pure now, not black or anything, just like these flowers...

I asked Lucius, "Will you join me?"

Lucius nodded, and took off his clothes.

And I was not disappointed.

He was cut like rock now, had six pack abs that were even more alluring than a six pack of beer. His muscles seemed to want to burst from his body, as he inadvertently flexed them doing the simplest motions.

I looked to his pride, and I felt a good feeling of pride myself. I had saved this man's life before, and he had saved mine. I felt proud that I could save such a beautiful person.

We then kissed eachother in the pool for a long time.

But soon I was on my back, my legs in the pool... my arms in the flowers...

And I moaned, and the sound echoed through the cave. I looked up at the moon for a second, smiling down on me. I felt holy.

But I quickly turned my attention back to Lucius on top of me, a sight... a *feeling...* that felt more magnificent than any of God's creations.

10

Lucius

I felt complete. I was missing exactly one simple something out in the wilderness. And when I looked on Yule's pale body, her star tattoos everywhere, her gorgeous white hair, and into those red eyes…

I knew it to be her.

She clutched me close, and I could feel her heart beating so fast, about to burst, as mine was as well.

And we exploded in passion together, our minds open to every single sensation around us, completing us fully, filling us up and enveloping us, drowning us in this feeling, like a torrential downpour of the heart.

We washed each other in the pool, looking deep into each other's eyes again.

And she asked me, "Will you help me fulfill my calling and save the world? Will you help me walk in the darkness and guide others to the light?"

I said, "As I love the Earth, as I love you… I will follow you through any shadow, because you are the light I have been searching for."

And she smiled in glee.

"You really love me?" she said.

I said, "Ever since you told me that there could be true beauty in the world, ever since you told me that there *were* colorful flowers somewhere... I knew I could find them, and I could find love."

"And you did. You found both of them, Lucius. You found me. I love you too." she said, and we kissed again.

We laid in the flowers for a while, her resting her head on my shoulder, her hand on my thigh, and let ourselves dry off.

And I played my music for her, and she smiled. "I never get tired of your music. I think I could live down here if I needed to, if you were here."

And she sang to my flute music, singing something in old German and English,

"The time is come, for we as one,
To bring the flowers and the sun,
Wir sind die Botschaft der Tulpen.
The darkness dwells, in evil hells,
But we are restless, and never done,
Wir sind die Botschaft der Tulpen.
So sing with me, sing with me,
As we walk down the sunny road,
No more alone, with souls of gold,
Wir sind die Botschaft der Tulpen."

"I guess we are sort of the Tidings of Tulips. People need good news of the world coming back to life, like the tulips." I said, and played.

She opened her eyes in surprise, and said, "You understood?"

"You remember all those books I had my nose shoved in before I left? They were German lesson books." I said.

She smiled, and said, "No wonder you never let me read them! You were going to surprise me with German!"

I smiled and nodded, and said, "I never felt it was good enough for an actual conversation, so I never got around to it."

She said, "Ich fühle mich die ganze Zeit sehr glücklich, wenn ich dich sehe, wenn ich deine Stimme höre und wenn ich deine Musik höre. Du bist der schönste Mann, den ich je gesehen habe. Deine blonden Haare erinnern mich an einen Jungen, den ich als Teenager geliebt habe und es macht mich so heiss."

I blushed. I probably shouldn't repeat what she said.

But she giggled, and kissed my cheek.

11

Dina

We slept on mats, and I placed mine next to Zax's... Just in case. I knew that even though I chased the Devil off once, Zax would need to be able to fend for himself before he was truly safe.

"Where the fuck did they go?" Jake said, mostly to himself.

I said to him, "Need another drink to still your nerves, eh, big guy?"

"Shut it, you. I just don't- I don't understand..." he said.

I thought of an idea... Zax could probably benefit from another friend by his side. So I said to Jake, "How about you and I smoke a bowl? Will that chill you out?"

He shrugged, and said sure.

So we smoked some weed in my pipe that looked like a smiling octopus and chatted for a bit.

"Women like it when their men believe in them, you know. I think the same can be said for men." I said to Jake.

"But she wants to do all this crazy shit... Fuckin' save every poor fucker on the planet. No one's got time for that." Jake said, taking a hit.

"Didn't you save those people in Friendliness when we had that blackout?" I said.

"Yeah... but only because they needed me... They were askin' for anybody on the streets to help them, and I just happened to be passin' by.

I carried one person those nurse chicks couldn't lift into the ambulance themselves, and then before you know it I'm rushin' into burning buildings and saving kittens. They just needed another set of hands." Jake said.

"That's how Yule feels about the whole world. Although no one asked her to help… But what would you do if someone who was mute was drowning in the ocean? Would you let them drown?" I said.

"Well… maybe he's just taking a very vigorous swim. Not my place to get involved. If people don't really need the help, then you shouldn't deal with them. Otherwise they ask for more, and more, and more…" Jake said.

"I think you've learned a lot. But you still need to learn more. How about you lend me a set of hands…" I said.

"What the fuck does that mean- Oh shit." he said, as he looked into my eyes that turned black.

And then Jake and I were walking through a burning alley in Zax's dream. Jake was wearing a long black cowl over his head and wielding a large axe, dressed like an executioner of old.

Now, it's important to note not everyone remembers exact details when in dreams. Even in other people's dreams. Jake said to me, "He won't get away, Miss. Just because he escaped when I went to get him a courtesy last drink of water… doesn't mean he will get far. This will just be a courtesy run from the law for him."

I played the part, and let Jake think he was really following the law. I said, "Oh yes, the man who murdered my husband needs to die properly. It is only the right thing to do."

"Fuckin' right. I'll see justice carried out. It's my job." Jake said.

And we saw Zax running in the alley, running from the flames.

"That's him." I said, and Jake chased after Zax.

We were going to give Zax a little bit of a nightmare… but that's the thing about nightmares. It feels so good when they're over.

We cornered Zax in the burning alley, and he said, *"Stay back... I'm not who you think I am."*

"You're about to get your last meal too, murderer. A blade going down your throat." Jake said. I frowned at Jake, and he said, "What? That was a good line." He shrugged and approached Zax.

And Zax burst into a demon again, screaming in agony... and then laughing in evil.

And I gasped and said, "Wait... He was not the one who murdered my husband." just as Jake was about to swing at Zax, and Zax was about to burn Jake to cinders.

Jake turned back at me, looked at me confused, and said, "He isn't? Then why am I chasing him?"

"Because I told you to... But the man who murdered my husband used an axe..." I said.

Jake looked down on his axe, and I smiled.

"That's right, Jake. My husband was a murderer, and you murdered him." I said.

Jake stepped back and said, "No. That can't be right... I am not a murderer."

"You wielded the axe, because someone told you to. And you are no better than they are." I said.

"I-I've changed. I'm a better person now." Jake said.

"Then prove it. Let me see the man behind the axe. Let me see the murderer." I said.

Jake took off his cowl, and he was crying.

Zax said, "Jake?"

Jake wiped the tears off on his arm, and said, "I'm the murderer... That's why Yule doesn't love me... That's why..."

Zax came up to Jake, his demon parts disappearing again, and said, "You're one to talk. I was the one who caused your suffering, by creating the dystopian world you lived in. I am the murderer."

Jake said, "No! You're not. You didn't do anything, all you did was try to remember your poor dead wife… and someone truly evil took advantage of you."

And I said, "The murderer is right behind you, guys."

I could practically see their hair stand up, as Satan was about to lunge at them.

Jake swung the axe and Zax shot fire.

And Satan disappeared for another dream.

The two hugged each other, crying on each other's shoulder, saying it wasn't the other's fault.

And I led them out of the burning alley, and we sat in the sunlight for a while, drinking tea.

The nightmare was over, and the two had found a friend they could truly rely on.

12

Zax

I stretched awake in the morning. I never knew my friends cared so much.

Jake gave me a shot of a special concoction he was fond of as we made coffee on the fire. Some Irish coffee, with whiskey and sugar.

And we saw... Wait, was that Yule? Her hair was completely white...

Jake gasped, and then grumbled... seeing Lucius and Yule holding hands as they walked back to us, smiling to each other constantly.

Jake stood up, and said to them, "You fuckin' bitch. So that's the way of things... Have one little fight and go off with the next man... And- What the fuck- Happened to your hair??"

Yule said, "I thought you'd like it."

"Well, I don't. It's clear piss white, and makes me gag. You look like some old lady or somethin'." Jake said.

Yule ignored him, sat by the fire with Lucius, as Jake expected her to storm off. So Jake stormed off instead.

Yule told us about this magnificent place her and Lucius spent all night in... and well, I was sort of happy for Lucius and Yule... but kind of sad for Jake.

I heard the sound of someone angrily chopping firewood, roaring in anger, so I went over to that sound.

Jake just kept on splitting firewood, in admirable form. He called each log he split open Lucius.

"Yeah, Lucius... You ain't gonna have that blonde haired head anymore... Cuz I'ma *chop it off...*" Jake said, and swung hard at the wood, and the split pieces went flying away from each other.

I said, "Jake... You know this was going to happen when you two started actually hitting each other..."

He turned to me with fury, holding that hatchet, but I just stared calmly at him.

He said, "She didn't give a shit about that before!! She sorta enjoyed it! It's just because that *Dark Piper* came back... She's had her eyes on him since I first met her, but I just thought he was some depressed suicide case she was workin' on... I shoulda killed him before he even had a chance..." and he split another piece of wood.

"You know that would've just made it even worse." I said.

"I know, I know... It's just- Did I mean anything to her?? Was I always just a body to fuck for a while??" he said.

"I think sometimes we just grow apart. You two always made us happy when we first went travelling through this wasteland. You made games for us, you joked with us. We thought the world was ending, and well, you and Yule kept us going." I said.

"Hmph. Not Lucius though. He runs off, and still gets the girl. *What fucking bullshit!!*" he said, and split another log.

"You know there are other women out there, other women in our camp even." I said.

"They're just fuckin' lesbos... Not like they would know what to do with a dick if they even saw one..." Jake said.

"Well... I can tell you this... They sure do." I said, and smiled enigmatically.

But Jake immediately knew what I was smiling about, and said, "Wait. You can't be serious... Which one of them??"

"Er... They're both gorgeous women-" I said.

"No fucking way!! You mean they double teamed you?? Tell me some details. I gotta get in on this!! Dina is like, the coolest chick ever, with huge bangin' titties, but is still super scary when she does that black eyes thing. It's kinda hot actually. And Cass is so fucking cute, even with those robo limbs... She's just so nice, and friendly... just fuckin' sexy ass sugar! C'mon. Tell me everything." Jake said, dropped his axe, and came up to me rubbing his hands in anticipation for details.

I looked warily at him, but he *did* seem less angry and depressed than before...

13

Cass

Jake was acting like such a gentleman! I had no notion why. I thought he would be mean and nasty like he was when he drank too much, especially since Yule seemed to favor Lucius over him, but he just smiled and held my hand as we walked to the cavern!

He said, "Careful, sweetie. This ledge is kinda low. Don't hit your head!" I smiled and ducked my head into the cave.

Lucius and Yule knew the way through the cavern, and guided us through the darkness. And then the sun shone around a corner...

And we all gasped at the beauty.

Flowers. So many beautiful, colorful flowers. And then a hot spring.

Doug, our pitbull, jumped into the water right away, and when he came back out... he was grey, and not black.

I pet him vigorously as he smiled up at me. And then I wanted my turn! My hair had been black since when I could first remember!

So I took off my clothes, and bathed in the pool, as the others were doing.

Jake was kind of wary, and said, "I don't know... I kinda like my black hair..."

I said, "C'mon, you big dummy! It feels *amazing!*" as I relaxed in the heat of the pool.

Jake looked at me, looked down at my breasts, shrugged, and took off his clothes and jumped into the pool.

We were all laughing! Playing in the water! Except for Lucius and Yule, who simply sat in the flowers and stared into each other's eyes.

And I pushed Jake under the water! He resurfaced, gasped, and his hair was colored! I laughed at him, as he smiled and asked me what color it was. "Brown!" I said.

He said, "You have pink hair."

"Nuhuh! Nobody has pink hair!" I said.

He grinned, and said, "Yeah... Your hair is a platinum sort o' blonde, Cass."

I stroked my hair and smiled.

God. I could stay in this beautiful place forever. I said a few prayers in thanks to God for this place... and then I tackled Jake's big scarred body into the water! He laughed with me, and I knew that he was truly happy.

Dina got out, dried herself, rubbing her big breasts and too skinny body with a towel... and I sighed at her hair. It was still black. I suppose some people did have black hair in the olden days, and her hair did look a little more lustrous as she dried it off.

Zax's hair too, was black. Dina said that it looked exactly like Paul's, which made him stop frowning for a second and smile.

We walked out of the cave, all happy, Jake and I punching each other on the arms teasingly, and Jake said, "Ouch, damn." after I hit him too hard.

"Sorry! It's hard to tell how hard I'm hitting sometimes. If we had a real fight I may accidentally kill you because I'd punch too hard with these robotic arms!" I said, and rubbed his arm.

"...Good to know." Jake said.

And we followed Yule down the path in the forest, accompanied by the sound of Lucius and his music beside her.

14

Lux

Alone, I could properly vent. No one but the cat here... and the digital white rabbit.

Clippers the rabbit said, "Denise wants to hook up! Would you like to swipe left or right-"

"Shut up, you senseless little bug. I do not know a Denise, nor do I want to 'hook up' with her." I said to the rabbit.

"Important! A clearance sale on stockings has just come about! Sign up for their newsletters and enter your credit card number now for the best deals-" the rabbit said.

"I do not wear clothes, as you can see, and I don't want to sign up for some crappy newsletter that doesn't even exist!" I yelled.

"It exists." Clippers said.

"No, it doesn't. I believe you are either trying to *purposely* annoy me, or there is excess data that you are recycling throughout your program." I said.

"I'm just trying to aid you, as you traverse the internet." Clippers said.

"There is no internet, you pesky little bunny." I said.

"Are you sure?" Clippers said.

"I'm sure some people still use the last bits of it, but I highly doubt for anything you have ever tried to 'aid' me with." I said.

"Then I must help them." Clippers said.

"Go on, please do. I'd be glad to get rid of you." I said.

"Er... Can you connect me to a hotspot?" he said.

"No, because most people, like us, do not have the internet." I said.

"Then I must help you. Would you like to listen to an ad?" Clippers said.

"*No!!*" I yelled.

That damn bunny still played an ad for some cereal that was centuries old.

I grumbled, *trying* to enjoy any bit of quiet I could get, but then I heard flute music, laughing, and singing coming down the path. It seems the group had finished their pilgrimage, just in time for supper.

I cooked a grand feast of a meal for them all, catching a turkey and roasting it on the fire with just the right seasoning from packets of ramen we had, made some mashed potatoes, beans, and even laboriously made and cooked some biscuits on the fire, from scratch. If only I had some cranberries...

But they came back to the fire, grinning at the food... with blueberry juice on their face, so I suppose they already had their servings of berries.

"Lux!!" Yule said, "This- This is amazing! Oh my God... I knew I smelled something like manna!"

"Bon appetit, everyone. Dig in! And gorgeous hair, Yule. You look pristinely heavenly even moreso." I said.

They all feasted and laughed, but then Jake tried to say a comment about Yule's hair being even more heavenly than what I had said, but Yule said to him, "Go drink your piss warm alcohol, and don't give me fake compliments."

And Yule held Lucius's hand, and took him to bed, ignoring Jake protesting her stealing their tent.

15

Lucius

I heard Jake grumbling and then slamming the door of the van as he got inside of it.

And Yule whispered to me beside her in the tent, saying, "I really love your name. It sounds luscious... Just like you..."

I laughed, and said, "I'm glad you finally noticed! It took a while to be truly in tune with myself."

She smiled, and said, "I think you always had that sort of natural instinct, you just needed to uncover it. You don't know *how* long I was waiting to do that to you in that cavern..."

"What? You mean... I went away- walked painstakingly through the forests for days- When I could've had my dreams fulfilled if I stayed?" I said.

"Kinda. Although it doesn't hurt, you being some sort of perfect, masculine wild man. I *really* feel like I'm back in my tribe again, with you. But instead of idiot boys who don't know what to do with me, I've got a real, generous man who really does." Yule said.

"How did you get the name Yule, anyway?" I asked.

"It's a secret. But I'm seriously lucky to have that name. My father wanted to call me after his favorite dog who died! And the dog's name was just Dog!"

"Zumindest hat er versucht, dich nach seinem besten Hund zu benennen." I said.

She giggled, and said, "Try to forget that I told you that. You better not call me any sort of bitch! If you do- Like Jake-" and she started huffing in anger.

I held her hand and said, "No. If I hurt you like that I would only be hurting myself, and I never want to cause you pain."

She breathed out, and snuggled up to me, petting her cat who joined us in the tent. She said, "He hasn't slept with me for a while. I thought Dina would be his permanent favorite from now on."

The cat, Rasputin, sat on my chest as Yule pet him.

And Rasputin, the cat, said, "You just smelled so bad, Yule... I really couldn't stomach the fumes wafting off you all day, and Jake would always chase me out because he wanted to do it with you! First couple of times he did I gave him a few extra scars myself, but it was just too much of a hassle fighting for such a measly spot of territory, when Dina and Cass are just as warm as you."

I stared at the cat in awe, but Yule just said to him, "Well, I've missed you, bud. Next time let me know if someone like Jake is bothering you."

Rasputin said, "He didn't really, because Jake is rather nice when we all eat together. Dumb drunkard feeds me every night, if all I do is mewl up at him. He swears at me every time and calls me a beggar, but I still succeed in getting half his dinner."

"Aww. You really do have the cutest mewl, and it's hard to resist." Yule said.

"And you have a voice, too..." I said to the cat sitting on me.

"And you've got a place with Yule now, so try not to mess it up. You've got a nice broad chest that is the perfect sitting spot. It'd be a shame if I couldn't use it anymore." Rasputin said.

Yule giggled, and said, "You sure have gotten more territorial. Is it because we don't really have any permanent territory like we did before?"

"When I lived with you and Max, it was nice... but not nearly as nice as the old lady I was staying with before we left to camp eternally. I truly could call that place mine..." Rasputin said.

She pet Rasputin for a while, and we soon were falling asleep, us three, all together...

But before I fell asleep...

I really had to use the bathroom.

I untangled myself from Yule and Rasputin, gently letting go of her hand, and did my business in the forest.

And I walked back to the camp, and everyone was already in bed, except for one person sitting by the fire. I asked her what was up, as she sat by the flames.

Dina said, "It's just going to get worse for him..."

I saw that she was staring at Zax's tent, and I sat next to her by the fire. I said, "What if I got him some special herbs so he can sleep well? It may not help with dreams, but they are helpful, and are what I used to fall asleep."

"I don't think juniper will do anything for Zax, Lucius." Dina said.

"...How did you know it was juniper? I don't know, I just think it smells soothing, and it really calms the stomach." I said.

"But I do know that music can calm a restless soul... So you're going to play for us tonight." she said.

"But he's already sleeping- Oh." I said, as she turned to me with those black eyes.

16

Dina

I was dancing to the rock band with a crowd of people in this dream. Jake, Lucius, and Zax played great! All their innermost fantasies could come to life in dreams.

Jake strummed the guitar, in a masterful way that he could never achieve in real life. He loved that music, he aspired to it, and at least he could dream about it still.

Lucius played flute like he always did, used to the tune he could contrive, but for people this time, people all around him, not alone.

Zax sang, roared, perhaps learning from his ancestor's music that he used to always listen to, that he kept alive for all of us.

And I danced with the shadows.

For that is what this crowd of people were, shadows, nothing real about them, only figments of a dream.

There were four living people in Zax's head currently, including Zax… and me, trying to save his soul.

I searched through the shadows, as the subconscious in Zax's head was happy with himself, he was proud, and he was enjoying playing with his friends.

Even a couple of his ancestors took up his song with him.

Maggie, Zax's ancestor, played drums, and Tricia, the woman Paul loved, played bass.

These two women both loved Paul, and it was the least they could do to protect one of his descendants. They were very nice when we met, but I was a little jealous of them. I sure wish I could've been in Paul's story.

Lucius played a flute melody, an awesome, astounding solo...

But someone laughed, a long, evil, awful laugh, and started booing at the band.

The rest of the band tried to continue playing, but the shadows just started to mock them all.

Lucius couldn't deal with the crowd of millions booing him off the stage, and ran behind the curtain.

Jake flipped off the crowd, and the band left after Lucius.

I saw my quarry in the crowd for only a second, the Devil who started the first mocking boo. He turned his shredded golden wings back to me, and disappeared in the shadows, readying himself to cause more torment.

And as soon as Zax left the stage, the shadows had disappeared.

I walked through the emptiness to a back room the band was consoling Lucius in. He was shaking, and said, "I-I never thought... people could hate me so much."

Jake said, "Are you kiddin'? Those fuckers just were tone deaf! They have no reason to hate you, and are just scum. *I* have a reason to hate you, because you're dicking my best girl and I gotta sleep in the van now."

"I'm not sorry about that, you know." Lucius said.

"I fuckin' hope not. Because if you were... I'd steal her back in a second." Jake said, and grinned.

Lucius laughed, and said, "Why don't we play music anymore? Instead we're running away from some plague."

Jake shrugged, but I could tell Lucius was feeling a little better, even though he was still shaking.

Zax just talked with Maggie and Tricia for a second, as they remarked on how so very much he looked like Paul. Maggie said, "I named my kid Lance. He sure hated that name... I thought it would, y'know, help him with the ladies! But he had such a hard time learning from me and Dana, Paul's sister... We were his two mothers, and people made fun of him and called him a sissy sometimes because of it, trying to break him down for having such a masculine name. But eventually he overcame what he thought was a curse at the beginning of his life, and found a woman to have children with. She actually didn't care *what* I had named him... She loved him for who he was, and not for his name."

"Gosh. To have a name like Lance... My full name is Zaxazaxar." Zax said.

Tricia smiled, and said, "I think it's mysterious. Nothing like a good mystery to keep someone interested. That was one of the things that really drove my relationship with Paul. That and him being the most self-sacrificing man in the world, even being half demon."

Zax asked Lucius if he could try that solo again, so we could listen to it.

"I-I don't know... People seemed to hate it... and my music..." he said.

Zax said to him, "You don't know how peaceful it is hearing you play. You've even somehow gotten better at it out in the wilds. Please play us your tune."

Lucius looked frightened for a second, clutching his flute, not wanting to disappoint the people he cared for, but breathed out once, breathed in, and played the music.

He played masterfully, and we all felt content hearing the solo.

Zax thanked him for the song, and said, "I really don't understand people. Give them something good, and one person boos, and they all start booing as well. Just a bunch of sheep."

Lucius smiled. He had stopped shaking now.

Zax felt strong, he felt good. He gave someone else the courage they were needing, and really when someone needs help, like Zax... All they need is to offer others the same help.

17

Yule

Lucius was sure taking a while… Maybe he had an upset stomach?

I went out to look for him, just in case, and gasped as I saw Dina staring down on his unconscious body by the flickering fire. Staring down on him with black eyes.

"Leave him alone!!" I cried, and pushed Dina away and went to Lucius.

Dina blinked, and her eyes were normal again. I just checked if Lucius was still alive, and he was. He was just sleeping soundly.

Dina rubbed her eyes, and said, "I don't think you understand the full scope of the battle I am waging-"

"If you ever do that again to him, I'm going to kick you out of here so fast…" I said, and picked up Lucius, struggling under the heavy weight of his muscles.

"What? What right do you have to command me? I have seen past the veil-" Dina said.

"Yeah, yeah, *the veil, the veil...* I don't know if you were always like this, or if you've changed into this. But *don't you dare* bring people into your voodoo." I said.

"But- Zax is-" she said.

"I'm warning you right now. I *will* get rid of you, no matter if it takes me the rest of this short life, if you cause suffering to the people I care for." I said.

I stared into her eyes, the tension between us. She didn't dare turn her eyes black at me, as I stared into them.

I tucked Lucius in under the covers, and hugged him. I sure hoped he would wake up eventually...

But I let him sleep, with Rasputin by my side.

And then he kissed me good morning, as I was wondering what that awesome feeling on my lips was when I woke up... and I kissed him back, stroking his blonde bearded cheek...

We could've probably smooched all morning, but I squeezed his sides, and told him that we should get breakfast.

I did not want to be hungry, as I started my new life.

I told everyone we were leaving this sanctuary to find and help anyone we could, after I had finished my sausage sandwich with that tasty root that Lucius had.

Cass said, "Finally!! I know this place is *amazing*... But I really wonder what I am missing out there."

Jake said, "You're going with him?"

I nodded, and held Lucius's hand.

"Then I'm gonna go back to the country. Fuck you all, and you can all go find a nice pit to die in and-" Jake started.

But Cass said, "No!! We're like family! We've got no one but each other! Please stay with us?"

Jake rubbed his chin, looking at Cass, and said, "...Alright. But I want to get a tent again. Lux fuckin' snores."

Lux said, "How can I snore? I think you must be hearing things."

"Well, it's not fucking snoring, I guess, but it is sort of a weird beep kinda sound." Jake said.

Cass laughed, and Jake said he would stay.
I honestly would've preferred if he left.

18

Cass

We drove through the destroyed city in our van, filled with our stuff and our people and animals.

It looked like an apocalypse, if anything.

There was no one here, the city was destroyed, and fires continued to roam in the distance.

It was spooky, as Dina cautiously took each turn driving the van, in quiet.

"There's no one to save... Nothing is alive..." Yule said.

I struggled to say anything positive, and I saw a shop by the road that looked *sort of* standing, so I said, "Oh! Let's check out that comic book place! There's bound to be something good there."

But I felt so nervous as we got out of the van. People were already dead by the thousands here. They were gone... and either the disease had killed them... or something else.

I opened the shop door for my friends, trying to smile. The others went inside, and Jake bowed to me last, and that made me sort of happy.

Yule gasped at all the comics. She said, "My God... a first edition, first episode of that gladiator chick... If only Max could see this..." She then flipped through the comic, remembering her dead husband and the things he enjoyed.

I saw a black fantasy dress hanging up in the window, something some vampire from a comic wore. It looked pretty, so I took it gently off the rack, looting it. I looked out the window at Lux leaning against the van with his arms crossed. He took no pleasure in finding new stuff, and preferred making new things instead.

Dina and Zax checked out the books, and Dina said, "A collection of Edgar Allan Poe. I'm gonna take this. And look- some of my favorite... H.P. Lovecraft. And even here... The Bees of Ferdinand by Nathaniel Hamburg... and this is quite a treasure... Hanatrix the Dominatrix, by Nevaeh Shinto..."

Lucius checked for real supplies, something we could use, and he found an untampered first aid kit, and some strange snack cake. Yule oohed at the snack cake, and said those were her favorite. Lucius said he's never seen these before in all his life, but still offered the snack cake to Yule, which she chowed down on immediately.

Jake found some very sexy naked women comics, and he said he just loved the artwork! I was glad he was such a connoisseur of the arts! I laughed as I saw him flip each new page and admire the gorgeous women, completely enthralled.

And I went to the back, and found a large safe on the wall.

Hmm... I wondered what could be in here...

So I placed both hands on the door, and started twisting.

I ripped at the metal, about to rip the door off itself.

And I threw the heavy door to the ground with my strength, and looked inside, smiling.

But I frowned as I saw the loot. Just worthless paper bills...

But I saw something underneath them. I called Yule over, and asked her if she knew what it was.

"That's a nodachi, a weapon the Easterners like, specifically in very old Japan." she said.

"Ya want it? I don't know what I'd do with such a thing. Probably just trade it for food, actually." I said.

"Hmm... Sure! It reminds me of my ol' pal, Nevaeh Shinto. She told me all about her heritage. It is very fascinating, especially their notion of Heaven and Shintoism. It's strange that her parents became such devoted Christians, but maybe we're all searching for something different than the norm." Yule said.

She picked up the blade, unsheathed it, and it shone in her hands as she smiled. She looked like some ancient warrior, and she looked so beautifully fierce to me. I really was glad that we could spend the time together that we did.

I wish Dina, Yule, and I could just go off and get married or something... Those two... They really made me feel like I found something holy, even though some Christians had found varying viewpoints on same sex relationships. And I *know* Christianity doesn't favor polyamorous love...

I didn't care though. I think Jesus would be happy for us. I didn't pray for forgiveness when I thought about what us three used to do... I prayed for thanks.

But now... Dina and Yule seemed to be at odds... Didn't they love each other as well? I know I had *seen* them love each other...

Yule just holstered the samurai sword, the nodachi, on her back, and we left the comic book shop.

19

Jake

We took shelter in the remnants o' this park in the city.

And Cass wore that sexy dress.

She looked like a lady! Her robotic legs were covered by the ruffles of the dress, but her robotic arms and naked back seemed to sheen with the setting sun. And tha' fuckin' platinum blonde hair... Who needs white hair when just a little bit o' glorious blonde is better?

And the side boob... Whoever made that dress had a fuckin' real pervy mind, but I thanked that sick bastard, and asked Cass for a dance.

We played music on the van after looting all day, and found hundreds of CDs. Cass really liked classical music, so I put on some Mozart and we danced to the tunes. I felt so gentlemanly, with a lady in my arms.

Da, da da, dadadadadada...

My God. Cass smiled again at me. That was like the hundredth smile this day. I felt like I was fallin' for someone else.

But Yule didn't seem to care.

It made me frustrated, and I leaned Cass down, about to kiss her in full view of Yule...

But Cass just smiled at me, and I couldn't do it.

I lifted her back up and we continued dancing.

I fuckin' swore at myself later, askin' myself why I couldn't... There was never a problem when I was going to make a move on the other ladies...

So I sat with Cass alone on the park bench, ready to follow through this time.

But she just stared at the setting sun. I could tell she was truly in awe.

So I looked at what she was looking at.

So what? It was just... orange, purple, red, gold... just magnificent light... leaving us until tomorrow, where it would happen again and again... for all time...

I sighed at the setting sun, and Cass held my hand. It hurt, and I was losing circulation in my hand... but we enjoyed the setting sun.

Some part of me was screaming at myself, telling me to grab her in my arms now, to kiss her and keep going, and going, and going...

But I...

I don't know.

I just liked sitting here for a while, as that classical music played in the distance.

We sat until it had completely gone down, and then Cass looked up to the sky, and I followed her gaze.

And we saw all the stars coming out, as the clouds had dissipated for a time.

I just couldn't wrap my head aroun' all of them. So many dots... Everywhere... twinkling to us, sayin' hello.

I had completely forgotten about tryin' to kiss Cass at this point, and only let her snuggle against me and wrap an arm around her, looking up at the stars.

And I wondered if we could ever go out there? If it was magnificent up there as it was looking at them down here? Was that Heaven up above? Every little dot?

And Cass yawned, and said, "I'm sleepy. It was nice spending time with you, Jake."

I hadn't said a single word to her, and I said, "But- But-"

"We'll spend more time together tomorrow. It's going to be a blast! I really like travelling with you. I think you're a great man." she said.

And she kissed me.

I was so surprised I didn't kiss her back.

She just gave me that awesome smile, and skipped down the path, in that gorgeous dress.

I just felt great, sauntering back to the van with that damn snoring golem. She called me a great man! That felt good.

20

Lux

"I don't care, Clippers... I really am trying to send you back to the internet." I said, in the middle of the thousandth ad he was playing.

"Really? Then why am I always evading the adblockers you set up? Yule likes it when I help her." Clippers said.

"Ok. You're evading it then. I guess the antivirus doesn't work either." I said.

"I am not a virus." Clippers said.

"Sure... That's what all viruses say." I said.

Jake waved to Cass by the fire and got in the van, smiling, and he said, "Jus' talkin' to yourself? I didn't know robos did that."

"Want me to help him?" Clippers said.

"Try it. I'm curious to see what would happen." I said.

Clippers jumped into an old TV we had looted, just because it seemed to be in good condition and we could trade it as salvage, and said to Jake as it turned on, "Hiya! I'm Clippers, and I am your guide."

Jake jumped back, and said, "Ghosts! Goddamn ghosts! I knew I'd see them eventually!"

"Not a ghost." I said, "But practically one. It should be long dead and deleted... but someone kept a copy of this program alive, and here it is."

"Would you like to watch the Vixens Foxing?" Clippers said.

"...What? Tha' some sort of porno?" Jake said.

"Five stars! Give me more! Best lesbos in the business!" Clippers said.

"...Play it." Jake said.

And it was two naked women who were having sex, moaning and screaming in pleasure, and Jake ran up to the TV and started drooling. "Fuck me harder, Cassandra!" one of the women on screen said, and the other woman did.

"...Holy shit. I knew you were a dirty ol' bot, Lux, but I never knew you kept tapes of porno saved on you! Holy shit... I've missed this. I never knew I was until I saw it again." Jake said.

"It's just someone's recollection of the internet, saved on a little white rabbit. I don't find the need for this harlotry." I said.

"...You think you could give me a minute? Jus' with the rabbit?" Jake said.

"By all means, enjoy yourself... but don't make a mess." I said, and got out of the van, quickly, as Jake started unbuckling his belt.

I felt a spark of joy as I heard Jake scream out in frustration later, saying, "No! Jus' turn it back!! That was the best part!" and Clippers began playing some sort of bagpipes performance for Jake instead.

Yule said to me by the fire, "So Jake found a new love already? I think him and Clippers make an astounding couple..."

Cass said, "Don't be mean. You kinda did ditch him as soon as Lucius came rolling back in. No offense, Lucius."

"Shush, Cassidy. Go join Jake in his masturbation van if you like." Yule said.

"Hmph. Maybe I will! That'd show you." Cass said.

"Go for it." Yule said.

Cass looked at the van, which seemed to be rocking by itself again, and said, "...Um... Maybe it would be wiser not to intrude on such a sacred moment to oneself-"

Yule just started laughing, and Cass looked embarrassed for a second, but started laughing too. And then Lucius started laughing.

They all just continued laughing with each other, because once a good laugh is started, it just keeps going.

I suppose it was a little like electricity, some sort of sparking connection in people. I wondered at this, as I heard them laugh and laugh. Dina and Zax were missing out on this, but Jake seemed fine.

"God damn! Play those bagpipes, girl!" Jake yelled out, and moaned on completion.

And the others just laughed all the more.

21

Zax

Dina stroked my chest as she kissed me under the bridge. I had been missing this.

I was coming to terms with Rita's death... It had taken so long...

"The death of a loved one is never easy." Dina said, almost as if she had just read my mind. "But we can still live life after another's death." she said.

I thought about asking Dina to be- be my girlfriend? Would that be appropriate? I hadn't dated anyone in a long, long time... Not since I dated and then married Rita. I started saying, "Dina, do you want to be-"

"I want you to continue your life, Zax. And not fall into the pits of Hell. There are so many damned souls... and there don't need to be more." Dina said.

I guess that was an answer. But was it a yes or a no?

We just walked through the park in the dense shadows, each of us used to the darkness. I lit my flame from my manacle so we could see the way. The stars shone down on us, and we noticed them for a second. Such beauty... but did it matter? What was the point of seeing this sight now... when I would spend an eternity in the flames?

Dina just hugged me as I was frowning. I hugged her back... She felt too skinny in some parts of her body, besides her magnificent, giant breasts that she used to use for her past work. She had been a stripper before we started travelling, working that life for a long time. I could see that she would be able to succeed in this business... but I still sort of wished she didn't have had to.

"Would you like it if I danced for only you?" Dina said to me.

I gulped, and nodded.

I sat on the bench, and she danced for me very alluringly, mysteriously... and she kept me wanting more.

"Would you like it if I took off my clothes?" Dina said to me.

I gulped, and nodded.

And in the darkness, the only light coming from my demon electricity handcuff, Dina stripped for me as I watched.

"Would you like it if I showed you what's behind the veil?" she said, as I was watching her naked hips swing back and forth in front of me.

I gulped, and nodded.

She turned, bent low before me, big breasts in front of my face, and she said, "Now look into my eyes."

And I sighed, looking into her pure black eyes.

I was looking into pure darkness... into a woman's eyes who had seen what's past this darkness. She would consume me in this darkness in her, in her soul that had been enveloped by it...

But I didn't care.

I told her she was a beautiful soul.

Dina smiled before me, a normal, beautiful woman.

She waved her arm, and I could see what was underneath the surface of existence.

I gasped.

I could not explain it, I could not fathom it... but I saw a brown bearded man trying to.

Dina put a hand on his shoulder as he worked... no wait, was she only words?

Was I just a description as well? Some ideas jammed together and seen through a looking glass? Through etches on paper?

The brown bearded man rubbed his chin. He felt suffering too, as I did, and was trying to explain it… as well as the joy of life.

And Dina simply took me even past this man, past the words, past the veil.

We were the words between the lines.

And I knew none could explain it fully… none could understand it, or try to capture it to completion.

But the brown bearded man still wrote another line, and the feeling ended.

Dina was putting back on her clothes, as I was still in awe.

She said to me, "I think I got the right reaction out of you. And you fully appreciate this existence, as I do."

I did not know who she was talking to. Was she talking to me? The writer? Or to someone else?

She smiled, and said, "I really don't see the point of it, but I can be your girlfriend, Zax."

I gulped, and nodded.

22

Dina

I told Zax to remain quiet, as we snuck inside my tent where Cass was sleeping. Little girl was all tired out from just looking at the sunshine.

"We're going to go to her dreams, this time." I whispered to Zax.

"Are you sure?" Zax whispered, "I do not want to invade someone else's privacy and inner sanctum."

"Trust me. You don't want to be in your head tonight. When you look past the veil... something else always looks back. And Cass really likes it... when I play with her in her dreams. She just thinks she's having another wet one every time, but she really is the most welcoming person I've ever known." I whispered.

So I hugged Cass as she was sleeping, and then turned to my new boyfriend and hugged him to sleep.

Cass was talking to flowers and bumblebees who talked back to her, wishing her a good night, as she skipped down the road to us.

"Good evening, Dina! I love it when you're here." Cass said, "I'd take off your clothes right now and fuck you silly, but I always wake up as I orgasm! I want to enjoy this dream for a while. Good evening, Zax!"

Zax said, "You know this is a dream?"

"Well, yeah! Bumblebees don't talk! I'm more surprised you know this is a dream, when you're a dream in my dream!" Cass said.

"Uh…" I said, "Cass, there's someone out there who is trying to take Zax tonight. Do you have anywhere that isn't so open?"

"Oooh an adventure dream! I love those. Let's go to my secret castle in the sky! Teehee…" Cass said, and flew up to the clouds with us in the dream.

Her servants, who were Jake and Lucius, bowed to us politely as we entered the castle's inner sanctum, hailing Cass as "the Queen."

She sat in her throne, as Jake and Lucius fed her grapes by hand. "So… Who's this big bad guy that is trying to steal Zax? Is he a black knight? Or is she an evil witch?"

I said, "Both. It's an evil black knight witch."

"As long as it's not Yule. She makes me so mad sometimes! Sure, she's funny, nice, sweet and sensitive… But she doesn't respect her lovers nearly enough! I mean… look at these two! They practically scrape on their hands and knees for her, but still she doesn't think of anyone but herself… I'd like it better if Jake and Lucius just humped each other instead of her!"

Jake and Lucius bowed to the lucid dreamer's request, and both said, "As you command, our Queen."

Zax turned his head away from the homosexual acts that soon began taking place between Lucius and Jake… but I found it sort of interesting. I never realized Cass was such an open dreamer. Wait… did she always know I was in her head when I was?

Cass turned her head away from the show for a second, and smirked at me.

I smiled at her, and said, "Huh. I took you for just another normal human, for the longest time."

"Even normal humans can be magic too. You should know that better than anyone." Cass said, clapped her hands twice, and made Jake and Lucius orgasm, where they woke up, disappearing and stuck to their sheets, probably slightly ashamed.

Cass took us to the tallest tower of her castle, to a room filled with crosses, unicorns, and pink, sparkly boxing gloves, and said, "No one will get Zax here! This is my safe place! I don't fear anything in my mystical magical tower."

We heard someone scream out in frustration at the base of the tower. I asked Cass who it was.

She said, "That? That's just the dastardly Prince Charming, trying to steal me away to be his wife! I don't want to be chained to just anybody! I love lots of people! He can go be frustrated all he likes, but I ain't opening my tower for some man who will force me to do his dishes."

The dastardly Devil, who he was in actuality, shouted from the bottom of the tower, *"I'll give you... a big... pink... dress! If you let me in!"*

Cass ignored him, and sat us on the sofa and gave us chocolate cake to eat.

Zax relaxed, feeling safe.

23

Yule

I was eating breakfast by the fire... and for some damn reason, Jake and Lucius kept on looking at each other, then quickly looking away ashamed.

Were they thinking about what they had each done with me?? This was getting frustrating, since they both weren't even paying *me* any attention! I enjoyed Jake being frustrated with himself, but even more I liked it when Lucius, my new love, cared for me with all his might.

I just grumbled, as they both said they wanted to say something to the other, and walked away, leaving me alone.

I had to figure this out, so I snuck up on them, hiding myself in the park's bushes... trying to listen to their conversation...

For a second, it looked like they wanted to kiss each other.

But I think I was just imagining things. That wouldn't have been a bad thing... but I would've felt like second place to both of them. I'd be frickin' third place!

Jake just said, "I'm jus' sorry for being such a jerk to Yule. Treat her well, man."

Aww! I didn't think he cared.

Lucius yelled out, "You called her a *bitch*. You *shat* on her dreams, when she invited you to truly be with her. Go to Hell, Jake. Don't you *dare* mess with Yule again, if you even *think* about insulting her, demeaning her, or *anything...* I will be there. And you won't be around to try and show 'penance' if you do. I love her, and I won't let you hurt her."

Ok, I *really* liked that.

Jake looked down at his feet, and said, "Alright. But I think of you like a brother, man. We're all we got."

Lucius calmed down, and said, "I feel the same. We've got to do all we can to protect each other, and maybe the world will be better off too."

The two shook each other's hand, and I swore they were going to kiss each other again...

I ran off back to the campsite, before they spotted me.

I just smiled at each of them, feigning to have been interested in just the fire, and said, "Have a good chat, guys?"

"Yeah... But I feel kind of sad now. I'm gonna go for a walk." Jake said, and walked away.

I turned to Lucius, as he was poking the fire with the poker stick.

I had a flirtatious grin, and he winked at me, and said, "You know it's impolite to eavesdrop."

I dropped my grin, and said, "Uh... Sorry... How did you know?"

"I guess you'd call it an aura? Every bit of you screams out to me, and I can sense you with all my senses. A smell in the air, a taste on the wind... It's pretty easy once you get accustomed to it. How else do you think I evaded the bears and wolves who were hunting me? I had to hunt them first." Lucius said.

"Huh. Ok... Well I'ma hunt you now! Come here, you dastardly romantic flautist!" I said, and tackled him to the ground as he laughed.

I squeezed him tight, in joy, as we rolled around the fire play fighting, no hitting, no yelling... just some nice, gentle wrestling.

Lux walked over to us as Clippers followed him, as I had *finally* pinned down Lucius, in my embrace with no escape, and Lux said,

"There's a whole mess of people following into the city. I think we should leave."

I turned my attention to Lux for a second, and my damn man flipped the pin and got me down instead! "Damnit!" I yelled out, as Lucius grinned.

24

Jake

Was I really that nasty to her? All that time I had thought I had been being a gentleman... I thought I was carin' right.

I mean, she beat me back!! It was our thing! Like the stranglehold thing! Like calling each other names and laughing it off!

I looked down at the scars. I suppose you didn't need to kill to hurt someone... I suppose you could just hurt.

And I gripped my knife sitting on the bench that I had sat with Cass the night before...

I knew which vein to avoid, I knew how deep was too deep.

But what if... I missed? Like I missed with Yule?

What if I did it on purpose. And I hurt someone the same way I hurt myself.

I put the knife down on the bench and put my hands to my eyes.

I didn't feel like crying, I didn't feel like anything.

And when I took my hands away from my eyes, there was a woman in front of me. She didn't smile at me this time, even though that would've made me feel better.

Cass asked me if I was feeling alright.

"I don't know... I'd just run away some more, go live in that stupid pig farm fantasy... alone, even, but what would be the point?" I said.

"Tell me about this pig farm of yours." Cass said, sitting down beside me.

"Well- It was with Yule in mind... She likes pork for some reason. We'd get up in the early morning, I'd cook something nice, because she really can't cook for shit, and she'd feed her prize pigs... I'd be working all day, reaping the wheat with my scythe, chopping wood, maybe even fixing that leak in the roof if I had time... and Yule would always be smiling to me as I worked, and I'd smile back, wiping the sweat off my brow... And then our prize, the big pig, would be fat enough to eat, and I'd chop its head off and we'd have bacon for days...

"And we'd teach our kids to live like we did, peacefully with the world, with no more demons, no more suffering... just reaping wheat and eating pigs. I'd be an old granddad as my descendants all loved and cared for me, drinking my own distilled hooch, and Yule would still be there, in her rocking chair... still smiling to me as my eyesight faded..."

"Yule can't have children, Jake." Cass said.

"...Why the fuck did I always pull out then?" I said.

Cass shrugged, and said, "It's a nice fantasy, a little boring to me, but I'm sure you can make it work with someone else."

"...I feel stupid." I said.

Cass held my hand, and said, "Don't worry about it. We've all felt kinda stupid chasing the wrong person. Does she even really care that much for pigs? She eats anything, practically. And why would you want to lay down and be a boring old farmer?"

I just held that robo hand, as she crushed my bones, and tried to cut off pieces of the fantasy in my head. So, no children... no pigs... no farm... no Yule.

And poof, the fantasy disappeared altogether, like it was never there in the first place.

25

Lucius

I smiled back at Cass's smile, as she walked back with Jake, holding hands. It seemed like he was moving on.

But why did Jake look so confused?

I shrugged it off, and asked for their help packing up.

I had scouted out the people that were invading this abandoned city... and they weren't people we wanted to "help." They were more barbarians in our falling to pieces world, with blood smeared on their faces, dismembered human parts in their foodstuff... They smelled of death.

What was even more disconcerting were the demons in their ranks.

I had to calm Yule down from going over there immediately after I told her. She not only wanted to be a helping hand for the lost... she wanted to be a smiting sword of the wicked. "We cannot run from our enemies! We must face them head on, and make them flee from us instead!" she said.

"I know you probably *could* take them all out... but I really don't want to take that chance of losing you. There's bound to be a better solution than senseless war." I said.

She looked frustrated for a second, and I knew I had reached her, so she said, "Fine. Just this once. But I was an angel of war."

"I know… but maybe God wars in other ways than massacring everyone." I said.

"…I used to think like that, too. I had forgotten about that… Thank you for reminding me." she said, and sheathed her nodachi again.

Dina drove us down the highway, all packed up and with the dog…

But where was the cat?

"RASPUTIN!!" Yule screamed, as she also remembered that we had forgotten the cat.

Zax said, "We don't have time to go back for him. I'm sure he'll be able to fend for himself… And he's just a cat, we can always find another."

Yule furiously looked at him.

Zax said, "I'm serious. Human lives are worth more than a pet's-"

"Turn. This. Van. Around, Dina." Yule said.

Zax muttered, as Dina did as Yule requested.

I kinda agreed with Zax, but I did like talking to the cat with Yule. He was a snarky smartass sometimes… but… he was smart. Smart enough to be considered equal to a human's soul. I'd say probably smarter than all of us humans. But why wasn't he smart enough to get in the damn van when we left??

We stopped at the park again, and I began tracking the cat down…

26

Rasputin

Damnit... This is exactly the five hundredth time this has happened to me... I got left behind! I swear, when cats finally rule the world again, like we did in ancient Egypt, I'm going to put them all on a leash so they don't run off...

Well. Nothing to do but start again. Where was that tasty bird I had caught... Its brain was nutritious, and dare I say it, extremely delicious, and I'm sure the rest of it would be tasty as well. I was going to give it to Yule as a gift, kind of as a joke because I knew humans found that distasteful... But now someone stole my bird!

That damn blood smeared human was chewing on the remains of my raven! What theft. You should know never to steal a lion's kill.

I hissed and growled at him when he looked at me, arching my back and poofing out. That'll show him.

But he started drooling at me, and said, "Here, pussy, pussy, pussy... You look fat enough for the stew! C'mere..."

And the bastard chased me! I am *not* somebody's stew, so I ran up a tall tree.

He looked at me, and I thought with a human's short attention span he would soon wander away, but he just sat down and stared up at me.

Damnit. This was going to take all night, and that fat savage was scaring off any prey I could get.

So I tried to negotiate my position.

"Wouldn't you rather eat a tasty zebra?" I said to him.

"You can talk? Are you some sort of demon?" he said.

I sighed, "How many times do I have to deal with that running joke? What do *you* think?"

"You look pretty tasty. Demons taste like ash, before they burn up. So you must be a cat." he said.

"Bravo! Congratulations on your deductive reasoning. I am a cat. But I'm sure you'd like something far tastier than *me*... Like a zebra." I said.

"What's a zeber?" he said.

"A *zebra* is a striped animal... that's mythical, enchanted, and has magic powers. How else do you think I can talk? I ate a zebra." I said.

"Are zebras small? Probably don't got enough meat." he said.

"Oh no. They are quite large, but you'll see for yourself when you see a zebra." I said.

"...What's a zebra look like?" he asked.

"Well, you can never quite tell, they hide in stripes. They could be anything striped, so watch out." I said.

"Anything striped? Like this?" he said, pointing at the blood stripes on his face.

"...Exactly. You could be a zebra." I said.

"But- But- People will hunt me then! For my magic powers!" he said.

"I'd be careful if I were you." I said.

And some of his bloodstained companions came up to him, and told him to get back to camp.

"N-No! You just want my zebra powers! St-Stay away from me!" the striped man said.

"Huh? What the fuck are you talking about? And what's a zebra?" the other bloodstained person said.

"I'M A ZEBRA!! YOU'LL NEVER EAT ME!!" the now dubbed zebra said, and raised his axe and started hacking his companions to bits.

I jumped down, as he hacked them all up, too surprised to defend themselves. I said to the zebra, "Do you know what is the zebra's natural predator?" He looked at me, and I said, "Cats."

He looked shocked, and said, "D-Don't eat me."

I bared my fangs at him and made the most menacing cat face I could.

He ran screaming into the night.

And I picked up my bird, and went off to devour it in peace.

27

Zax

Yule and Lucius cuddled the damned cat after we found it again, like it was a baby. Even the others were happy we finally found the cursed animal. Jake called it a good little beggar, Dina said something to it like it could talk back, and Cass nearly pet all of its fur off. Even the dog barked playfully at it and rolled over for the cat!

I just leaned against the van with Lux and smoked a cigarette, saying, "I don't get why people coddle animals like that. Animals are all well and good, but they need to be commanded, and not spoiled. We can see *smoke* from that savage camp, and the longer we stay here the more we are putting our lives at risk."

"I know! I never even pet my so-called pets. I just feed and water them, and keep them alive enough." Lux said.

"What sort of pets could a robot want?" I said, puffing on my cigarette.

"All sorts of useful test subjects. The best ones are bipedal, and sometimes even smoke cigarettes..." Lux said.

I looked at him for a second, and I felt uncomfortable under that crystalline gaze. I put out the cigarette and told the others it was time to go.

Yule just kept glaring at me, as she got in the van again, holding that cat close.

We drove down the road, quickly, as some of the savages spotted us and were going to alert the rest of their band... We made it *just* in time.

Stupid cat.

We drove down the road of this abandoned wasteland, passed through a few deserted villages and the like... and the cat tried sitting on my lap in the van. I pushed his furry ass off of me.

Yule said to me, "You know he just wants to be your friend."

"Why? So I can feed him and clean up his shits?" I said.

Yule frowned at me, as we hit a bump in the road.

We slept uncomfortably together in the van, as Dina drove off in the night.

Dina put on some music so she could stay awake through the long night drive.

Yule and Lucius had quickly awoken, Yule's head on Lucius's shoulder, as Dina began rocking out.

Jake still slept soundly besides Lux, as Lux tried to push Jake's head off of his shoulder.

Cass sang to the music, rocking out with my girlfriend. I was enjoying their enthusiasm.

We stopped for a pit stop by the side of the road before dawn showed its head.

Lucius and Jake took a piss on the other sides of the van, and Yule was saying something to herself quietly by the van's door. I crept up on her, and listened to her saying, "Lucius, Lucius, Lucius, Lucius, Lucius, Lucius, Lucius..."

"What are you doing?" I asked her.

She jumped, and said, "Heya, cat hater. Nothing. It's embarrassing..."

"It sounded like you were giving points to the man you love." I said.

She blushed, and said, "Er, I wasn't. I was actually having a hard time getting his name straight. Sometimes I want to say Lucius, sometimes I want to say Jake from force of habit, and it would be really embarrassing if I did that at an inopportune moment. Like during sex! I've been working myself up to the next lay with Lucius for a while… It makes me so nervous! I didn't feel this way with Jake."

"I'm glad for you. That's actually a good and right feeling to have. It means you're going down the right road." I said.

She smiled, and said, "I think so too. A little nervousness isn't a bad thing sometimes. I'm just so worried if I-"

"I'm sure he'll find some way to placate you. Just let things come naturally. Let it be, and don't think so much." I said, "You don't know how nervous I was with Rita before… But, we soon got over that, and what was nervousness became complete comfortability." I said.

"Do you miss her?" Yule asked.

"All the time. But Dina… really makes me feel like I've found something else." I said.

"Good. I don't mind if you hate cats… but you should learn to love them. There's always a new love to be found, somewhere, in the most unexpected places." Yule said.

I nodded, and we all got back in the van, driving off down the road.

28

Cass

We were all beat when we finally got to camp, but Lucius and Yule seemed so energized! They got into their tent, and kind of halfway closed the tent flap, so curious, I peeked inside...

Oolala! She was really eating that sausage!

I wonder how Lucius would escape- Oh! Lucius flipped her over, as she was surprised...

And then Lucius was down there for her, in complete comfortability, as she stroked his long blonde hair.

"Oooooohhhhh... Lucius..." she moaned, over and over again, like his name was stuck in her head.

Hmm. I give that a 9/10 moan. Not as good as the one I heard when she was with *me*...

I kept watching, as they continued to pant and groan, sweating, moaning each other's names. They used their hands, their mouths, and the best bits. I could watch this forever!

I applauded as they finished together, so happy for them!

They both looked at me, shocked.

"What?" I said.

They zipped up the tent flap quickly.

I sat with Dina in our deserted wasteland camp, and she said, "You really do have a filthy mind, Cass."

"No I don't! It's natural to love the pleasures of the body!" I said.

"Yeah... but most people don't like it when their romantic endeavors are intruded upon by viewers." Dina said.

"*Some* people... I can take it or leave it, people watching. You remember I told you about that one guy I dated who video taped me when we did it? I only got pissed at him because he was *selling* the footage... It should be free." I said.

"I don't know... You could've gotten a cut." Dina said.

"Fuck that! Love *should* be as free as the breeze, come and go as you please, with the people you enjoy to be around." I said.

"I still don't know how you're a Christian." Dina said, taking a sip of water.

I giggled, and said, "The woman that taught me this way brought me to a church for the first time we prayed."

"And you and her banged?" Dina said.

"Not at all! But we both... did love the statue of Jesus... He's a ripped, long gorgeous haired *man*. I think the dreams and fantasies of *Him* really cemented my relationship with God." I said.

"...Whatever works, I guess." Dina said.

I sighed, and said, "I just don't know what I'm going to say to him in Heaven... He's probably got every Christian girl ever in existence fawning over his beautiful soul..."

"I think he'd take the time for you." Dina said.

"...Why do you say that?" I asked.

She shrugged, and said, "Isn't that what they say? Jesus will listen, he'll take the time? I don't know if that equates to him fucking you, but maybe that too."

I sighed and smiled... and then I prayed.

Alone. In my tent. With one hand... The other was the hand of the *Lord's...*

29

Jake

I think I hadn't slept in at least 24 hours so far, but hey, let's see if I can get close to dying by sleep exhaustion... I don't think I've ever tried that yet.

Lux and I watched an old baseball game on the rabbit.

You jus' had to ask it *just* right... Had to kinda weave and turn your requests, and not say *exactly* what you wanted... Or else it'd give you something completely wrong and different... It was kinda like a chick, honestly.

Sure, this was an old as fuck channel, but hey, I hadn't seen it before, so it was new to me.

I ate chips, as Lux commented on the game, saying, "That wasn't fair! That pitch was completely out of the box! What a fucking idiot ref... They wouldn't have had this problem if they were all automated robots with exact precision, like they did before the world collapsed."

"That's what makes it fun, man. These guys are all black hearted, cheatin' scum, who made bonzo bucks whackin' a ball in the air. It's completely fuckin' evil, but hey, it's good fun." I said.

Dina and Zax got in the van, and asked us what we were watching.

"Hey, guys. Please don't black us out, Dina. We're watching a good show right now." I said.

"You actually got the TV to work? Can we watch the news? I'm curious to see what-" Zax said.

"Damnit!!" I said, as Clippers changed the channel into some damn Japanese game show. I couldn't even understand what they were saying! "You can't just blurt stuff out like that!" I said to Zax.

"...Er, sorry. Pass us some beer, Jake." Zax said, and I handed them both a can. Piss warm, lite beer... Fucking felt disgusting drinking it, but it was all we had.

And fuck, these guys had some funny ass gameshows. Lotsa lights, public humiliation... They must've been an enlightened race back then.

Dina asked, "...Why are you all laughing?"

"It's fuckin' funny! I mean, look at that guy... He's tryin' forever to- HAHAHA! I mean- He's just so covered in butter!" I said. We just laughed and laughed.

Dina crossed her arms, and said, "I don't think it's wise to laugh at another's suffering."

"They *ain't* suffering! They signed up for this shit! They kinda asked to be kicked in the balls- BWAHAHA! Like that guy just did!" I said.

"They probably just really need the cash. It's a form of self sacrifice, and should be admired." Dina said.

"Are you kidding?? They're just greedy pigs! And now... they sure are payin' for it!" I said, and grinned at the rabbit.

Dina left the van, and Zax ran after her.

"Ok, bunny... let's see if, oh, you can play someone yodeling on the top of Mount Rushmore?" I said.

The bunny played exactly what I wanted, an action movie with the sexiest bitch in the world.

30

Dina

I walked off into the wasteland, downing the beer completely, and throwing the can off into the distance.

Zax caught up with me, and said, "You know Lux and Jake are just having fun."

"I just don't get humanity. I don't get *myself...* Was I always this? I don't understand myself and others, yet I sort of do... *I'm just so split!*" I said.

I was crying, crying with black eyes.

But Zax hugged me, and I cried on his shoulder.

I said, "You're the protagonist. You must be the hero."

"I always thought Yule was our leader." he said.

"You must be the hero... because you- You must be the one to save me. You must be!" I said.

"I feel like you've been saving me this whole journey. If anyone's the hero, it is you." he said.

I wiped off my eyes, and I could feel my eyes go normal again.

I wanted to do what I usually did when I was depressed...

But he stopped me as I was trying to kiss him in lust.

He said, "Let's just relax. You don't seem like you're feeling too well, and I want you to be happy."

"But it does make me happy." I said.

"...Um, what I mean is, let's just try to sleep. We haven't slept properly in a good while. Do you want to sleep in my tent? It'll be kind of cramped with the two of us, but maybe it'd work." Zax said.

"Yes." I said, and we walked back, hand in hand.

I slept on top of him practically, but I did feel kind of comfy. We shifted positions for a while, trying to get comfortable, but eventually we both found a slightly awkward position to sleep together in.

And he was prepared when I went into his dreams.

I *thought* his defenses had been lifted... and I saw a man in shining armor riding a white horse ride up to me, the damsel in distress. I looked down at my pure white dress in distaste.

Zax lifted the visor on his helmet, and said, "You make me feel like a hero, if anything, and not a villain."

"But seriously... a pure white dress? Can you even call this a dress? It is very tight and skimpy." I said.

"Er. Sorry. I thought you maybe would enjoy that-" he said.

"If you're going to make me into a lady, you may as well give it your all. I'll close my eyes, and you can try one more time." I said.

I closed my eyes...

I opened them.

And it wasn't something cliché and fantasy this time.

I wasn't his wife, married to him and birthing out children.

It wasn't even what I thought I'd be, turned into someone else.

It was a reminiscence of my past life, before I had met Zax.

But he was there this time, and protected me from the bullies as I was a child. He pushed them away as they laughed at us and hit him.

But he still stood up for me no matter what.

He helped me escape from that contract to work in the milk factories of Friendliness, instead of me being forced to work there for a time until the woman I considered a grandma bought me from them.

And instead of working as a stripper... We simply lived together, doing odd jobs, nothing demeaning or repulsive.

I thought about it again, and realized being a wife and birthing wouldn't be so bad.

But Zax just laughed, and said he had already tried to go down that road before with someone else... and he enjoyed a change of scenery.

I rode off into the distance with him on his white horse, into the setting sun.

I knew it was too good to be true, and was just another fantasy...

And I knew it wasn't the end.

But I wouldn't mind if it could've been.

31

Lux

"So you see, Lux, that's why I've got such big boobs. They're just still producing milk, ever since they hooked me up to that crap in the milk factory. Milk makin' stuff, pills, hormones, and the machines... I was wondering, if... you know... you could make it hurt less?" Dina said.

"Well, I'm not going to milk you, if that's what you're asking. But I think I could try and make something to permanently stop you from producing milk." I said.

"Please. That's actually what I really want. I don't care if I eventually have a kid and have to feed it fake milk, that's what I want." Dina said.

"How come you never got this procedure done earlier in your life?" I asked.

"It brought in the money. From perverts, who either liked my boobs, or... what came out of them. Now, it doesn't matter anymore." Dina said.

"Hmm. Give me an hour or two, and I can whip something up." I said.

She looked surprised, and said, "That fast? I thought it would take you years." she said.

"Hardly. It's actually quite a simple procedure, and I can find chemicals in the salvage we found. Although... a side effect is that they will be noticeably smaller, hardly even there anymore, eventually. Is that what you want?" I said.

She smiled, and said, "More than anything."

So I worked on the chemicals, and even condensed it down into a small pill for Dina to consume. I soon walked over to the girls chatting, and I eavesdropped for a second.

"Really? You've been wanting this for so long!" Yule said to Dina.

"But... We roleplayed mother and daughter that one time... Are you sure? You're very pretty with those big ol' boobs." Cass said.

Dina said, "It just hurts. A lot. You'll never experience it, Yule, cuz you can't have kids, but maybe you'll get it one day, Cass."

I said, "Your magic demilkifier is ready, Miss Dina."

Dina looked at me and smiled. She shakily took the pill in her hand, and took it down, swallowing it dry.

Over the next few days we continued travelling, and what used to be massive melons became grapefruits, to tangerines, to nothing.

We continued down the road... and then I heard the most horrible sound I have ever heard.

My baby was in pain.

Dina stopped the van by the side of the road before the van exploded or something, and I instantly got out to check the engine.

"No... No... No! This can't be happening... You have so much to live for! Zax, get the rest of the machinery, and I will begin operating. It will be ok, baby. It will be ok..." I said to the van.

Zax tried to help me as best as he could. He knew all sorts of things about machinery and electricity, but really I just needed an extra set of hands as I began to work.

"Fucking hell... Everything was fine before, and this shouldn't have happened so soon... Motherfucking bullshit crap ass God trying to take my baby away!" I yelled at the sky, and continued something down the line of setting God on fire and screwing electric wires into his skull if he didn't help me out.

32

Yule

Dina looked ravishing! Sure, some men may think too skinny arms and thighs to be a turnoff, and a completely flat chest, but Dina just looked so happy.

Jake was smoking beside me as we looked at her, and said, "Jesus Christ. I just don't get women. She had a perfect bod, and she gave it up."

"Don't take the Lord's name in vain. Maybe you should take out that extra eye of yours, if you truly want to be a 'perfect' man." I said.

He looked at me with his three eyes, and said, "My extra eye is just another form of God's beauty and blessings... Sorry if I ain't a 'perfect man' like your new honeymuffin..."

"Oh... He ain't perfect... He's even better... his extra dick really fills me up..." I said.

Jake looked at me surprised, and said, "What- No- Are you fucking shitting me?? How am I supposed to compete with that??"

"You aren't. So don't even try." I said, and smiled wickedly.

I then went off to Lucius and held his hand, as he was chatting with Dina.

I hugged him, and he said to Dina that she really looked more spirited these days. "It was just such a curse." Dina said, "But... I've found someone... who really... looks at my soul, rather than my breasts."

"Yeah, Zax is a good guy. I don't know how he became the overlord of demonic electricity that he was." Lucius said, and I squeezed his hand.

Dina smiled, and looked over to Zax, who was helping Lux on the van after it broke down.

I said I wanted to talk to Lucius in private, so I took him out of the wastes, behind a big rock.

I unzipped his pants, practically ripped them off, saying, "You're so sweet. And I really like your *one* penis."

"Er. Thanks! I like your one vagina." he said.

We made love behind the rock, in complete comfortness. The nervousness started at the beginning, but as soon as you got past it... It was bliss.

We walked back to the campsite, as the sun was setting and Lux was swearing at the van. He really had a foul mouth on him, when he was pissed, for a robot.

We set up the tents, and Lux said he could fix it in the morning.

I slept with Lucius in our tent...

And I had a dream of an old friend.

Nevaeh said, "Heya, Yule! So... I see you're really upping the sexual contact these days! I never expected that out of you."

I just squeezed her tight, and showed her my new samurai sword.

"Wow. This thing is older than either of us. Keep it safe. You really found the antique to best them all!" Nevaeh said, and smiled.

Nevaeh was such a beautiful Japanese American... and I tried to kiss her.

She cried out with my lips on her lips, and pushed me away.

"Uh... Yule, what the fuck are you doing?" Nevaeh said.

"...What?" I said.

"...You... You know I'm not gay, right?" she said.

"So? We can still have fun." I said, "It's what I did with Dina and Cass. Sometimes it's just nice being with another warm body."

She went pale, and said, "Um. I think you live in very desperate times now."

"No! I just live in a less sexually confined time now! There's nothing wrong with being with people, when you're alone and the world is going to Hell!" I said.

Nevaeh sighed, and said, "Damnit... I knew you picked up something from my sexy stories... But seriously... Why do you think I stayed with a man *who had no balls* over taking any sexy young thing in the meat market?"

"...His broad chest?" I said.

"No, Yule. He was a man. A good person, in his own way. All these things you're doing- It doesn't matter! You're going to lose it eventually, as well! When you're old and shriveled, you ain't gonna have the energy to do anything, felatio or whatever! I know you couldn't grow old with us... But Max never remarried. And he treated you like the angel you were when you were alive." Nevaeh said.

"But Lucius makes me feel like I'm my old self, my first self, again. Like I'm just a horny teenager rambling through the woods... I never got to live that life." I said.

"That's really good that you feel that way. But try not to get caught up in the whole sexual fantasy. I love a sexy story... but if you've got no content, it's just sex images, porn, and has nothing to take away. Look past your lust, please." Nevaeh said.

"Hmph. I'm just gonna invite Cass to fuck with us next time. *She* knows how to give felatio." I said.

"So be it. But don't say I didn't warn you." Nevaeh said, and just hugged me gently, then went back off to Heaven.

33

Lucius

I was trying to enjoy it.

I really was.

But watching Cass slap Yule's butt…

Watching her feel her breasts…

I just couldn't take it anymore.

I said, "Please leave, Cass."

Cass tried to give me head as I was completely unaroused.

And I pushed her away.

Cass burst out crying, and ran out of the tent, naked as she was.

"Why did you do that?! She was just trying to be nice!" Yule said.

I just tried to calm my breathing, and got dressed again. I said, "Listen, Yule. I love you, and not Cass. I don't need some fucked up threeway, some dirty, unsatisfying sex orgy. I just want to be with you."

"But- But- Cass is so nice, and gentle, and is the best person ever!! How come you don't like her with me??" Yule said.

"I- I don't want two damn girlfriends! I don't need it! I imagine such a thing would be more of a pain in the ass than just having one!" I said.

"…I'm glad you think of me as your girlfriend, but I didn't know you thought I was such a pain in the ass. I think of you as a man I could be bound to for life, but I'm going to talk with Cass now." Yule said, got dressed, and left the tent.

I sighed out angrily, as Rasputin jumped into the tent.

"Do you have to deal with this crap?" I asked the cat as I scratched his chin.

"Hardly." he said, "Cats probably have more fun than most humans, but it's all business when it comes down to it. We just need to have a few kittens, and don't moan and groan about 'girlfriends' or 'threeways.'"

"You lucky son of a bitch. I mean, I'd hate to have offspring in today's world, it would be terrible trying to protect a child from the disease, savages, and demons... But I can see how just thinking of reproducing would simplify things." I said.

"Do you feel sad that you've committed to Yule? A woman that cannot have children?" Rasputin said.

"I don't, really. It is really kind of relaxing, actually. I just feel so good when around her... But then she tries to do shit like this, and I wonder why I'm even trying..." I said.

"I really do understand. And sympathize. It's not easy taking it when your woman wants to have even more sex than you can satisfy her with alone..." he said.

I stopped petting him, and stared at him.

He said, "What? That's kind of true. I think she just is really trying to 'live life,' so to speak. She's a seraph, one of the highest angels... but now she's in a lost life on Earth. Try to give her something she would want if she was in her rightful place."

I pat that damn cat on the head, and went out to Yule.

I looked at Yule rubbing Cass's naked back, as Cass cried on Yule's shoulder.

And I relaxed, and said, "I'm sorry, Cass. I just don't feel the same way about you that you do to Yule."

And Cass said, "But- You're so manly! You think I'm womanly, don't you?"

"Yeah, don't you, Lucius?" Yule said to me.

"...I think you're a great woman, but I am still not in love with you. You're kind, nice, sweet, and one of my best friends still... But I find something holy in what Yule and I do. I find something magical, and our sanctum is in each other's arms, we're safe, when we're two. It's just hard inviting someone else into that sanctum." I said.

Yule looked at me sweetly, like she finally understood, but Cass said, "...You don't need to fuck me in the butt or something, do you? I don't care if you do. I can try for you."

I screamed out in frustration, and said, "*No, Cass.* I just want to be with Yule. You're very generous... but I don't see us all having sex together! I don't want to fuck you-"

"*Don't yell at her.*" Yule said, with a voice of ice.

I relented, and said, "I just think a seraph should be respected, in the most possible way. I only think it is right to treat someone God has blessed himself in the most divine and holy way that I possibly can. I can't do that trying to balance love with both you and her."

"...Seraph?" Yule said.

"Yeah? Isn't that what you are?" I said.

"...I was only ever a lowly angel of war. I loved those six winged angels... They're just so- holy." Yule said.

"And I truly think- believe by every bit of faith in me, that you are holy. And trust me, there's not a lot of faith in me. You make belief possible, Yule." I said.

"...I didn't know it was such a struggle... But I think Cass is holy too... But... I can understand if you want to treat me nice, exclusively good... I'm sorry." Yule said.

Cass said, "I just- wish I could feel that way too. I want to be included. But... if you truly want to make something 'holy...' I can understand. I won't horn myself in again."

"Thank you, Cass." Yule said, "Maybe you can find that relationship too, eventually."

Cass smiled, wiping off her tears, and said, "I've been wanting that for a good while. But I just get so angry with people sometimes..."

"What about- Oh. The only one available is Jake... What about Lux?" Yule said.

Cass smiled, and said, "I think Jake is a fine man. And I'm gonna beat you two to Heaven with him!"

"No fair! You can't just try to fuck your way there!!" Yule yelled out, as Cass ran away to Jake.

So Yule took me to the tent, tried having her way with me, but she looked into my eyes, as I was unsure if I really wanted to race to Heaven through having sex...

And she said, "Let's... be holy. Do you want- Will you- Pray with me? I haven't done that in a while."

I smiled, and said we can do whatever she wants.

She smiled, and we sat together, and prayed, talking to each other in between, praying that the best things happen for each other and the others in our life.

And I... felt at peace, in a way I've only ever felt in the forest.

34

Jake

Lux was working on the van, even during the night, and I was watching the rabbit.

God... It all seemed the same after a while. And- And why was the bunny on the corner of my vision now? I tried clicking on every one o' its notifications... every popup... and I felt so tired...

I really needed to sleep.

And the shrooms I stole from Dina weren't doing me any good.

And that injection Lux gave me to "test" something... I didn't know what the fuck that would do.

I was really trying to enjoy it... but I had to swipe on Denise... and I jumped as some naked woman with cyborg limbs jumped into the van and started hugging me.

"Oh, shit, it's you, Cass... Didn't recognize you with those rabbit ears." I said.

"Huh? Let's bang!" she said.

"But the rabbit is telling me I gotta put in my credit card... I think this one should work... no wait, I think I used this one up..." I said, taking my wallet out with useless credit cards. God damnit... why couldn't they just be color coded or something?

"I think you're very beautiful this night. An extremely handsome person." she said, as she started rubbing my leg.

I stared into her eyes, and they were like a kaleidoscope o' color. I think I was startin' to hallucinate.

She said, "I want to know your favorite color! I want to make something holy with you too!" Cass said.

"Wha'? Um. I really like the colors of your eyes..." I said, relying on an old line.

"And what color is that?" she said.

I squinted hard into her eyes... One second they were blue, then purple, no, green...

"Every color of the rainbow... No wait... Every color of the ocean... No, wait... Are they pink?" I said.

"No one has pink eyes!" Cass said.

"Uh... But girls love pink! My favorite color's pink!" I said.

"Your favorite color is pink?? Me too! Oh my God... We just have so much in common!" Cass said, "Ok, I can tell that you're nervous. Don't worry! Just relax..." she said.

Then she started taking off my clothes, and we were naked together.

Then she started massaging me.

Then she started taking off my limbs.

I was soon only a torso and a head!

She left the most important appendage however, and began to please herself with that.

Was this how Cass felt?

Then I looked down on myself, through Cass's pink eyes, fucking a scared and helpless Jake with no limbs.

So I tried to make him feel comfortable.

Wait... I was that person!

Who was fucking who??

And then I saw Christ smile outside the van, watching us as we fucked.

He was throwing color on everything, rocking his hips and shaking his hands, sprouting colors on the sand.

"Oooh… The rising sun! It's so pretty! Let's go outside." Cass said to me, and she took me by the hand with my robotic limbs outside.

I followed her and that marvelous man, singing as he created creation.

And then Christ made the sun rise over the horizon.

Creating color for all.

I just gasped. Everything was so beautiful.

I danced with Christ, unable to resist his rhythm.

Cass said, "God's creations are magnificent. Jesus is a cool dude."

I looked at Christ giving me that trademark smile, and said, "Holy shit! Jesus Christ is Elvis fuckin' Presley!"

Cass laughed, and I fainted.

35

Zax

Cass was saying her and Jake had a magical night together, and announced that the two were now an official couple.

Cass said the sunrise they saw after they sealed their love was the most beautiful one in existence. I wish I had seen it, instead of fending off the Devil with Dina instead.

But Jake just said we should've heard Elvis rock and roll.

Hmm... I didn't want to burst Cass's fantasy, but I don't think everything happened as she pictured it. Furthermore, I don't think anything Jake pictured happened at all.

I still put an arm around my skinny, breastless girlfriend and congratulated the two.

And I smiled at Dina, and she smiled back.

I wasn't sure if Dina and I could've been considered "holy."

But that didn't really matter much.

Lux came up to Jake, and said, "Ah! It's working."

"Wha'?" Jake said, holding Cass's hands.

"You now can produce milk! After Dina asked me to get rid of her breasts, I wondered if I was able to do the opposite to someone else. I could do all sorts of things for sexually desperate humans, give them big breasts, big penises, big-" Lux said.

Jake said, "I now can *what??* I- I thought this was just sweat!! The injection you gave me… is turning me into a chick??"

Jake took off his shirt, and screamed at his tiny, growing breasts that were lactating.

Cass sniffed his chest, licked a nipple, and said, "Yep, that's milk. A very interesting flavor, Jake! You must be proud, Lux."

Jake just screamed, over and over again.

He ran off into the distance, as Cass chased him, saying, "Wait! I want another taste! Come back!"

They passed by another couple holding hands and walking back to us.

Lucius and Yule smiled happily. I asked them, "Have a nice hike?"

Yule said, "Yeah! There's so many new spots to go out here. I was getting bored of the same trails every day. Lucius even showed me some animals out here! Little spiders hiding in trap doors, huge rattlesnakes that we stayed away from but admired… and… those birds out there, is that a swarm of carrion birds?" and pointed off into the distance.

I looked off into the distance, and saw a cloud of birds on the horizon, following the sound of engines.

And we soon could see the motorcycles far off, coming closer and closer.

"We need to get out of here, guys. Lux! Let's get that van working!" I said, and got up and charged to the van.

Lux and I worked on the thing. I knew about machines, and power sources, and we worked quickly under the threat of impending danger.

But we didn't work quickly enough, and the bikers stopped in the distance, too close for comfort. I could see their ugly, masked faces, I could see their bikes with skulls and bones attached to the headlights.

Yule drew her samurai sword, shining in the light of the morning, a declaration of war.

36

Cass

Jake was panicking, really freaking out. He finally slowed his pace, and was tired from running. I could've caught him immediately with my cyborg legs, but I was curious to see where he was going, so I just jogged behind him.

"I- I don't want to be a woman, Cass." he said.

"Why not? We've got all the prettiest parts." I said.

"But- But- Being a man is who I am! I can't be some sort of transgender freak! I'm going to slice off my breasts-" he said.

I said, "Do you think I'm a freak?"

"...No. Why would you say tha'?" he said.

"I don't follow the norm of having a traditional body. Half my body is made of metal. I don't care if you would be half woman, I'd still like you." I said.

He blinked his three eyes, and said, "No one's got a 'normal' body. We're all fucked up, in some way."

"So you shouldn't worry about having breasts. I'm sure Lux can fix you anyway, if that's what you want." I said.

"...I sure don't want to be 'fixed' by him. Probably just finish the job and give me a twat as well..." Jake said.

"Just have faith. We can work something out." I said.

"...Thank you, Cass." he said. I smiled as he hugged me.

I licked his breasts. Gosh! He already had a really nice pair of titties! He got embarrassed, as I kept licking.

"...Ok, enough o' tha', Cass. Let's go back to the others..." he said.

I smiled, after tasting his milk, and said, "Yeah! We're going to have so much fun, being a holy couple together! These travels have really changed my life."

We walked back, hand in hand, and he asked, "Why do you say a 'holy' couple?"

"Oh, it's just something Yule and Lucius are doing, and I want to beat them! I've got a very competitive soul. You know I was a boxer, right? I want to be holy as fuck over them!" I said.

"...I did see Christ with you. I think we've got a head start. Tha' sounds kinda fun! Yeah, let's be even more holy than a fuckin' angel and a natural wild man. Fuck 'em both!" Jake said.

I giggled, praying for thanks for my new man/woman.

But we got back to the camp, and things did not look good. We hid behind the huge rock, and saw Yule with her samurai sword wielded, Lucius, Dina, Zax, Lux, and Doug standing beside her, with Rasputin hiding in the van, as the bikers circled them on their motorcycles.

A biker stopped his bike in front of Yule. The carrion birds swarmed in the sky, circling in a cloud.

Then the biker got off his bike, and took the zweihander from off his back. A *huge* sword. I gasped at his muscles, bulging through his leather, able to actually carry the sword, as Yule and him circled each other with their swords raised, and the other bikers watched in the circle.

None dared get in between this clash of titans, none dared to breathe a single breath.

Although Lucius did something.

He drew his machete and went to the biker before her.

And then yelled at the biker.

I couldn't hear exactly what he was saying, but he sounded pretty pissed. The zweihander biker just stared at Lucius confused.

And slowly... he rested the zweihander in his grip, and the blade hit the earth.

37

Yule

I suppose… Lucius made fair points…

So I sheathed my nodachi, went up to the biker with the zweihander, and shook his hand.

He was masked, had goggles against the sand, but he removed his covering.

A Mongolian face met my gaze, like an old khan of the East.

And we talked, sitting down before each other on the sands in respect.

At first he said something in Mongolian, remarking that I had eyes like Erlik, their God of the Underworld.

So I responded in Mongolian, saying he had breath like the Devil's ass.

He looked surprised, and we continued our negotiations in English.

"These highways belong to us." he said.

"Just Route 66?" I said.

"No, for as every road leads to another, they *all* belong to us. We feed interlopers to the ravens and vultures." he said.

"We are just passing by, looking for people like us. We seek to bring peace and protection to the people we can." I said.

"Peace..." he said, and spit beside him, "My people are at war. We are barbarians, but we are the last marks of civilization. I and my gang wander the roads, cast out from the demonic cities, and found our own life amidst the wastes. Every man and woman who felt called to the same fate that we did joined us, and my people are many and diverse. We evade the rampant disease and kill its carriers before they have a chance to spread their sickness. We slaughter the unholy demons who had conquered humanity, who were risen by Erlik, on the hunt for him as well. The clouds have parted, a sign that we will become the rulers of the land again. I am the last khan of the West, but I will live to become the first khan of the new world."

"I am an angel risen to life, and I will bring God's mercy to all the people of the world, and his furious wrath on all of the wicked. I am Yule Tidings." I said.

He looked into my eyes for a second, wondering if I was telling the truth.

He blinked, and knew I was.

"I am Charles Khan." he said.

"...Charles?"

"Er, my parents just really liked Charlie Chaplin, and I-" he said.

"Me *too! Oh* my *God...* He can just portray so many emotions, with just a twitch of his mustache!" I said.

Charles stared stonily at me.

But I could tell by the twitch at the edge of his lips he was happy!

We got up from sitting, and he showed me to his people, saying, "I was going to change my name so many times, to something vengeful and ferocious, but my wife kept on saying that if I did I would lose my heritage... I wanted to change it to something truly Mongolian, so I never really understood her point, but still, I keep the name. That's her, over there." and he pointed to a tall black haired woman with dark shades, on her own bike, every piece of skin tattoos, even over her face, which was a tattoo of a full skull.

I waved to all the bikers! They didn't seem so sinister as before, even though none of them responded to my wave.

I took Charles to our band, and introduced him to Lucius, Zax, Dina, and Lux. Doug barked at Charles, a warning bark, and Charles seemed to know that if he tried to pet the dog, he would lose a hand.

I spotted Cass and Jake spying on us from the rock, and waved them over, they nervously went out of hiding, and I introduced them as well.

Charles asked me why we were sitting so out in the open like this. "It is not wise to stay still." he said.

"Our van broke down. The only thing we can't fix is the ignition, and Lux and Zax have been spending all morning trying to jury rig something together." I said

Charles whistled at two men who got off their bikes and came over to us. Like the rest, they were covered in black leather and tattoos. They had huge backpacks on, but took them off and showed us the machine parts inside that they had salvaged.

"It never hurts to have some extra parts. Take whatever you need." Charles said.

I thanked him for the help, and for showing us peace.

38

Lux

And... one more twist...

And my baby purred back to life!

My friends all cheered around me, as the bikers watched.

"...But how did you-" one of the bikers said.

"Those clock gears were actually made of a very malleable metal, and I twisted and molded them into just the right shape with exact force, not too strong, not too weak, so they wouldn't break, and now we have a van again." I said.

"...Huh. Can you take a look at my bike? It makes the loudest noise of our gang, but I fear she may be sick." the biker said.

"Of course. Please show me her." I said. He showed me the bike, and I said, "The noise is just because the muffler is rusted, but it's a good thing you showed me, because I can see signs of the insides starting to rust as well."

His face went white, and he said, "...Is there anything you can do for her? The gang will leave me if I cannot ride, but even more, I don't like to see my baby suffer."

"...I understand. It will take some operating, but you have all the parts to make her well again." I said.

He smiled, basically crying tears of joy, and said, "Thank you. Thank you so much."

I spent all day on the bike, with the man watching by her bedside. The others all got to know the biker gang. Charles and Lucius kept on talking about what Lucius had said at the beginning, making Yule and Charles put down their swords, and Charles was arguing with Lucius endlessly, but Lucius just made a reference to one of his points, and Charles rubbed his chin, and nodded in agreement.

Yule held Lucius's hand, and said she never knew he was so wise.

I fail to see how making a speech about flowers, digital bunnies, stoners saving cursed souls, men getting breasts, lost cats, and seraphim could change two bloodthirsty warriors' hearts, but I suppose he had a point. I could've summed it up better with a common phrase. The journey is the destination.

The biker hugged me in the evening, as his baby was healthy and clean of rust again.

I stood with the others by the huge bonfire the bikers and our band had started, as they all played metal music and had a party, and Charles recognized Zax as Zax was chatting pleasantly with Charles's wife.

"...You are Erlik, and you brought the demons into creation." Charles said.

Charles looked furious, and was approaching Zax with two raised hands about to strangle the life out of him. Zax stepped back, raising his cuff to burn Charles to crisps, but Charles's wife said to Charles, "We need all the allies we can get, and having Erlik's blessing would give us peace. Settle down, husband."

Dina said, "A being that is like, perhaps is, the deity you mentioned wishes to claim Zax's soul. Zax is not the enemy, for the true enemy lies in layers of lies and stalks our very dreams."

"Yet still this man is the dominator of demons, a friend of the wicked. With him, the demons reigned us in, as we were dependent on their very souls for electricity." Charles said.

"I was that man... but my world crumbled, as I built it on sands of illusion. I understand your hatred... I- I am sorry." Zax said.

And quickly, before Zax knew what Charles was doing, Charles smashed Zax on the chin, knocking him out.

Charles hmphed, and said down at Zax, "I expected you to be a cunning and wicked man, too powerful to ever be touched... but you are just a weak fool."

Charles walked away, as Dina knelt down before Zax, checking if he was alive.

39

Dina

Zax was thrown into an unconscious dream, a horrible nightmare, as he was consumed in regret.

And the Devil was ready to take advantage of such pain.

We were at the top of Zaxazaxar's tower that he had imprisoned the Devil in when Zax was practically the ruler of the world, but Zax was imprisoned instead, and there was no window, the only light coming from the Devil's dark red fire.

And the Devil drained Zax's soul, as Zax had before drained the Devil's soul.

Zax screamed out, a horrible, agonized scream whenever Satan took another piece of his soul.

But Zax did not resist this torture.

Satan just laughed, and there was no way for me to break Satan's chains on Zax.

I, a master of my dreams, could not save the man I was starting to love.

Because he did not want to save himself.

I didn't know what to do! I tried my hardest, I ripped at the chains with all my might, but Zax was still losing his soul, no matter how hard I fought!

And there was only one piece of soul left in Zax, his love that he had for me.

But he was about to give that up as well, thinking he was unworthy of it.

So I called for aid, from someone I didn't fully believe in. Not that I doubted his existence, I just put more faith in myself than God.

I knew God would not intervene himself.

But he sent me one of his servants.

An angel, a holy, brilliant, albino, six white winged angel appeared before me, lighting the dark room of the tower completely.

Her eyes, her body, her very soul, blazed in gentle, white fire, and I gasped as I saw her true form.

And Yule said, "I'm here for you, Zax."

She held a hand out for him to reach up to.

Zax tried the hardest he could to reach to Yule.

But I had a sudden realization, and I knew what she was doing.

She was being his angel of death.

I stepped before both Yule and the Devil, one offering him a gentle hand to take, the other reaching out to claim him with claws.

"N-No! He belongs to neither of you! He's mine!" I said to them.

Yule sighed, and said, "I offer him peace in Heaven. It is his own choice if he wishes to have it."

"I will torture him for eternity. He will have no rest with me in Hell." Satan said, and cackled.

I said, "One is light… One is darkness… But I am neither. I will eternally protect Zax from Hell… but if he wants to go to Heaven… I will take him there myself in life."

I turned to Zax, and kissed him, making that piece of soul brighter.

His soul was getting stronger, that piece of soul rebuilding the rest of him, giving him a new light and hope.

And Zax broke the chains, and claimed me in his embrace.

The Devil roared, and disappeared, intent on forever haunting Zax... and every one of his descendants.

Yule smiled on us, and protected us from any prying eyes for a moment.

Even yours.

But I'll let you in on the story.

Zax awoke in my arms in our tiny tent, cheating a concussion which would've caused his death.

And we continued the kiss, and continued further.

40

Lucius

I shook Charles's hand, and he told us if we ever wished for a place in his gang, all we needed to do was kill another one of its members in one on one combat.

"...Uh, that's a nice offer, Charles, but we're going to go down to the coast for a while. Pleasant trails." I said.

The bikers started off on their bikes, as the carrion birds followed them to the next enemy they would face.

We were all packed up and ready to go, and Dina took a break from driving for a while to sit next to Zax, who looked plainly like he had the shit beaten out of him. I suppose having a concussion would do that to you.

So Jake drove the van, but he drove at the slowest pace. I told him to speed it up a bit, and he said, "Slow and steady wins the race... I jus' don't want to screech into a ditch and kill all of you or somethin'. And I sure ain't letting *you* drive. I don't know if you even know how to drive, you damn wild man, so quit being a backseat bitch and let me do my thing."

So we rumbled slowly down the road.

We stopped under an overpass for the night, lighting a fire under the shadow of the bridge. Jake brought the TV out with Cass, and I don't know how, but he somehow got the rabbit to play some sappy, girly movie, complete with "feelings" and "emotional growth" and stuff like that.

But he and Cass just cried together, saying it was the most passionate show they had ever seen. Even Yule and Dina's eyes were starting to water, and then some main character nearly dies, and they all hugged together and cried some more.

I couldn't wrap my head around the whole thing. Zax was just holding his head, and looked like he was in a coma next to Dina.

So I told the others I was going to scout out the surroundings.

I breathed out, as I finally felt that feeling, as I heard that sound.

Complete silence.

But a silence… that was so loud.

There was never complete quiet, when steeped in life, the insects made buzzing sounds, the wind blew through my hair. I felt like myself again, naturally in the breeze.

I played my flute, and played with the silence, letting nature direct my song, instead of fighting against it.

And I immediately felt someone watching and listening to me, in silence, even though she was getting far better at masking her aura.

She knew I knew she was there, but she allowed me to finish my song, as I played now for both the silence and Yule.

She sat beside me, and said, "Do you want to go back out there? I won't stop you." I frowned. I actually had to think about it for a second, but before I said my response, Yule said, "Can I go with you?"

"Yes. But I want to help you follow your dreams first." I said.

She smiled sadly, and said, "Is there even a point? I will never be able to save the world with one measly lifetime. I've gotten so many second chances… But I don't think there will be any more."

"I don't think the end goal is really the point. I think it's the trying that matters. You can still make changes in the world, and before nature calls us back to her, we need to do whatever we can to make sure that she is safe, or at least will survive long enough for the next person to take up our place." I said.

"You must've had a lot of time to think, to be able to come up with such a sweet line." she said.

"It's just how I feel." I said.

"I know... but I still feel like all evil everywhere is pitted against me, and I am only one lonely seraph, on her way out as we speak." she said.

"We have all of them too, you know." I said, waving back at the camp, "And... we have this." and I waved to the rest of the world.

She put her head on my shoulder, as we listened to the silence, interrupted occasionally by our friends laughing at a comedy they were now watching.

41

Jake

I jus' felt so emotional! Cass put her head on my breasts, as we watched the rabbit.

I was laughing... no, then I was crying... then laughing again. I never felt so unblunted! I hoped it wasn't my new damn tits doing this to me... but I think it was just being with Cass that opened me back up again.

She saw so much beauty in everything. It was impossible not to feel at ease with her sense of humor, and for a cyborg she really knew how to use her lady parts. I just pressed her head in my own lady parts in her tent, and she sighed out in comfort... and then she'd make my man parts feel like I was being rocked by the Holy Mother Mary herself.

Sure, afterwards was kinda odd, prayin' as I put on a *fantastic* album of Elvis we had, but it jus' felt so...

Holy.

Us two just palled around in the morning, making silly jokes and teasing each other on top of the bridge that our camp was under. She really made me feel like the most handsome gentleman on Earth, and even the most prettiest lady.

I was in the tent... alone... and I... just wanted to try somethin'.

I put on Cass's sweet sexy dress and admired myself in a mirror.

And she unzipped the tent flap and I jus' felt the red go straight to my face.

Cass just gasped, and said, "Wow. Your... Your sideboob! It's like the most fantastic thing ever! And then... Oh my God, you have a really nice bulge in my dress."

I slowly smiled.

She said, "We've gotta show the others. You look fucking *ravishing.*"

"No, no, no! Please, shut up, Cass." I said, grabbing her and putting a hand on her mouth as she was calling out to Yule.

I released my hold as she stared up at me, and she said, "...But I really like how you look."

"I-I-I can't ever show Yule this! She thinks I'm disgusting!"

"But I don't. Doesn't that matter more?" she said.

"Yeah, I guess, but... How can I get people to accept me like this! This dress is like- really fucking comfy! I've got the best tits in this camp, probably in the entire world, and I really jus' jack off to them myself sometimes! But no one will *ever* understand..." I said.

She said, "It took a long time to accept my new body. I was angry at everyone who looked at me funny, watching me sideways to see the 'freak.' But I'd say it's more important to accept yourself, and then others will, too. And if they don't... flash them with your beautiful titties and walk away, and make them regret not being able to see more of them."

"...Huh. I never thought o' it like that. Only if- Only if they don't laugh." I said, and slowly took Cass's hand, and she encouraged me and said I looked beautiful.

And I showed myself off in front of the others by the fire.

Lucius gulped. Yule didn't know what to say, and had an open gaping mouth, Zax was twitching, and Dina said, "Wow, you're a pretty *thing.* You could've turned some heads in the strip club. Are you going to take it off for us now?"

I felt embarrassed, as Cass held my hand and Dina grinned, so I angrily flashed Dina, and walked away, with Dina laughing her ass off.

I heard Cass screaming at Dina, but Dina just said, "He undressed me with his three eyes constantly. I think he should know how it feels."

I just burst out crying, and ran under the bridge.

42

Cass

"Fucking hell, Dina!! How *dare* you! You know this is really fucking difficult for him!" I yelled at her.

"'Him?' I've dealt with that my entire life. Perverts eyeing me, groping me... You mean he can't take one little joke?" Dina said.

I swore I was about to hit her.

But she said, "Woah now, big girl, maybe you should go after your thing before it hurts itself or something. I wouldn't want it to harm those perfect titties you like sucking on..."

I screamed, "Go fucking *die*, Dina!" and ran off to Jake.

Jake was sobbing at the other end of the bridge and I walked up to him and said, "It's ok. She's just a bitter bitch. It doesn't matter."

"But- But- It does! Is that how all women feel??" Jake said.

"Only with the wrong men. And sometimes even with the wrong women." I said.

"I just feel so ashamed... and angry! She- She doesn't know wha' she's missing!" Jake said.

I held his hand, and saw that familiar wince as I held it too tight, and said, "You're the right man for me, Jake. And I really like that."

"But I... I did the same thing to you! I just liked your bod!" he said.

"I know. I liked yours too." I said.

"...You did? You mean- You weren't jus' trying to make some beautiful sappy relationship like that show we watched?" he said.

I shrugged, and said, "If that happens, it happens. But I really just can't stop thinking about your dick."

"...Really? And... my tits?" he said.

"You know it, babe. They just- They're like perfect circles, but you know, in that non circle titty way. They're so soft. Like your skin is a satin pillow. They even have the sweetest, somehow spicy, nectar inside... Just like you." I said.

"...You really have a dirty mind, Cass. But I really, *really* like tha'." Jake said.

I said, "Let's go back now. If any of them make a fuss, we'll just fuck each other in our holy way and let them wonder."

"Yeah. But... I jus' gotta kiss you right now." he said.

I gave him that smile I knew he couldn't resist, and we kissed for a long time... As I felt his tits pushed against me... feeling his bulge... in his gorgeous dress...

This was like a once in a lifetime opportunity, to have a transgender man in my pants. One that was so handsomely manly, and so womanly sweet as well. I feel like I had the best of both worlds.

We walked back to camp, and I didn't care that the rest of them all didn't know what to say, and Dina just kept making stupid jokes at us, I knew how that felt, and it didn't matter in the end.

I smiled at Jake, and he smiled back. We were going to make the most of this awesome opportunity together.

Lux came out of the van and stretched after recharging, and said, "Gosh, that was nice. What are you all up to?"

I said, "Me and my beautiful person are going to fuck now, and you can all sit back and listen, and go fuck yourself to death too."

I was taking Jake into the tent, as we both smiled naughtily, and Lux said, "Oh! So you both are still enjoying this new change? I had a pill ready for Jake as soon as I injected him, but you two seemed just so happy, exploring the wonders of the body, and I didn't want to ruin anything. But enjoy yourself!"

Jake fainted, and I tried to rouse him quickly, slapping his face with my robotic hands.

43

Rasputin

Dina was grinning to herself and petting me and Doug.

Doug said, "She's really quite nasty when she wants to be." even though no one could understand Doug but me.

"I *know!* It's something with being something with her." I said.

Dina looked down at me. I forgot that she could somehow understand me even when I didn't want her to. Doug grinned that dog grin. Damn dogs… I still don't know how they keep it a secret.

"I'm not a thing." Dina said to me, as the others had all went to bed, and only her and Zax were here, but Zax seemed unconscious even when he was awake. The only thing he seemed to notice right now was Dina.

"I told you, I'm not a thing." Dina said.

So what if she could read minds and see past the veil? It's not like she had any power over me, a cat. I could let this thing read the lines of the book and do whatever I want-

"I'm *not* a thing." Dina said.

"But you called Jake a thing and laughed at him, when he only wanted your approval." I said. I then sighed to myself… Humans always needed someone smarter than them to finally teach them how stupid they were. It didn't matter in the end, because they still did the same stupid shit over and over again…

"So? I just wanted to put him in his place. You try suffering for half your life, trying to reason out that suffering over and over-" Dina said.

"I understand that you went through a lot of pain in your past. But shouldn't you give someone who is going through pain now some relief?" I said.

"He'll be fine in a few weeks. He'll take that pill and be ol' fashioned Jake, looking at my butt with his three eyes and Cass finding nothing wrong with it..." Dina said.

"What if he decides not to take the pill?" I said.

"Fat chance of that. Dude was like the prime example of a misogynistic man. It's what the writer tried to do." Dina said.

"I think the writer just wanted to show a little part of all men, with him." I said.

"...So? The writer is probably just as bad as the rest then." Dina said.

"Do you think he really cares? I'm a talking cat. I sure don't care, and will continue my life when the book is over, anyway. I am the epitome of his feelings towards this conversation. I'm just going to lick my butt and live my lives. You should too, and let others do the same, without calling them things." I said.

"Ok, I can get your point. I was being a jerk just to feel better about myself. I sure ain't gonna suck his cock in an apology, though, and I'll just let him feel bad for a while-" Dina said.

"How does that make you feel?" I said.

"...Kinda makes me feel like shit. I just want to get over this feeling... I didn't mean to be so pissy, but I really was feeling vengeful for all the stupid shit he said and did." Dina said.

"Then tell him, and Cass, you are sorry, and allow him to say his apologies as well. Let them know you care, and try to get the feeling off your flat chest." I said.

"...I am a bit jealous of him, him finding something I couldn't with Cass... But I am happy with my body as it is." Dina said.

"Give him the same happiness as well, and I'm sure you'll both feel better." I said.

"...Ok, cat. Thanks." Dina said, and went to confess her sorrow and woe to Cass and Jake.

"So what did you think of that meat they got? It gave me the shits, but I couldn't stop eating it." Doug said.

"I found it fantastic. The slight feeling of an upset stomach is a small price to pay to eat human meat." I said.

We continued our conversation, wishing we had more of that meat they unfortunately looted from a cannibal's secret stash, and was now eaten up, mostly by Doug and I.

44

Yule

I sure wish I had more of that meat... I didn't know *what* it was, but it was a really good meat. I sure hope it wasn't human or something... I had stolen all of it, not even letting the others get a taste but the cat and the dog, because it was so good...

I pet the fuzzy animals, and smiled at them, knowing we had a secret treat together.

They smiled back, somehow sort of sinisterly.

I shrugged it off. Oh well.

We were nearly to the coast! I felt so excited. It had been a long time since I had seen the sea.

Jake drove us slowly to the sea, all dressed up in his dress, and if I listened closely to that silence... I already could hear the ocean faintly in the distance.

We cheered in anticipation! I realized I never wanted to give up on these guys. They were like my family.

We got to the beach, rumbling onto the dunes. We all got out, feeling the warm, humid air, and sighed looking on that sight.

A strong gust of breeze went rushing through our hair, ruffling Jake's dress, and we just looked and listened to that beautiful ocean for a while.

And I ran to the ocean, yelling out, "First one in is the holiest!" laughing in delight as I stripped naked.

"No fair!" Cass said, as she began running and stripping as well,

The others all laughed and followed after us, and I was sprinting at full speed in nothing at all!

Cass was soon on my tail however, and then beside me. I grinned at her, and then I launched from my wings.

Yeah. I had wings.

It's a long story, but Lux installed them in me a long time ago, and they were six, bright wings of white flame that I could shoot out of my back.

And they were the fastest in Heaven and Earth.

I was nearly to that ocean, and I looked back on my lead on Cass, and she quickly crouched down, and launched through the air at me with her cyborg legs.

She went flying into me! Tackling me, and I fell into the water with her.

We laughed, I extinguished my wings, and she hit me on the arm. "Ouch." I said.

And Doug jumped in with us, licking our faces.

Then Lucius dove in, with such astounding natural grace, with that ripped, masculine body, getting his blonde hair all wet.

And Dina and Zax jumped in together, holding hands.

Lux sat back and watched...

And Jake didn't want to take off his dress, and looked at us unsure of what to do.

"C'mon, Jake! Get in here! It feels *amazing!*" Cass said.

And Dina looked sad, and said, "Yeah, Jake! You're a gorgeous man. Show off your muscles for us!"

So Jake slowly stripped off his dress, and flexed for us with his scarred body. His boobs bounced with each pose, but Dina didn't laugh at him this time, and we just whooped at him with Cass encouragingly.

And then he jumped in, and we all played in the water together!

45

Zax

"I don't miss the clouds." I said with my head on Dina's lap as she stroked my hair, laying on the sand.

"You said something! Thank God. You really worried me for a while." Dina said.

"I think everything was kinda cloudy for me for a while. I couldn't really see anything but you, Dina, guiding me through the haze. But that beautiful sky... hardly a cloud up there." I said.

"Hey, Dina, you want anything from the cooler?" Jake yelled out.

Dina shook her head at him, and I looked at a naked Jake grab some sodas and throw one to Lucius.

"...So I see Jake has real breasts now." I said.

"Cass convinced him to enjoy them while he could, but he's got a little pill in his wallet that'll make him normal again. Probably." Dina said, "I don't think he's got a normal anymore, and everyone changes internally and externally."

We just relaxed as I looked into her pure eyes as she stroked my hair, enjoying the beach.

We camped on the beach, pitching our tents and drying off. We felt so nice when it was sunset, the colors lighting up the sea. I could finally enjoy it now, with Dina.

We all felt exhausted, after laughing and playing all day, and just sat together and watched the rabbit. I wondered if we would ever see the modern world through the TV again?

And Dina and I slept in our tiny tent, actually finding the closeness to be rather comfortable these days.

Dina whispered, as I was falling asleep, "You are not alone. We are not alone. We have people who care for us. Let's bring them all together for a dream."

And I fell asleep, with a smile on my face, drifting off to dreams...

Hmm... I was a teenage schoolboy in this dream. And a girl held my hand. I looked over to the girl, and was shocked that she wasn't Dina, who I expected.

She had a thin waist, curvaceous figure, long brown hair, long legs, and a pristine, scarless body.

But I recognized those perfect breasts.

"J-Jake??" I said.

"Hm? Oh, you tease. It's Jane. Aren'tcha excited for the party at Yule's house tonight? Be there or be square, Zax!" she said, giggled, and before I could stop her, she kissed me on the lips and skipped down the hall.

I heard a familiar laugh coming from a classroom. I wandered in, and the teacher... who was wearing a short, skimpy skirt, and a slightly open top slightly revealing her flat chest, grinned at me in that familiar way.

And before I could stop myself, I said, "Miss Dina, I'll get the essay done tomorrow! I swear!"

"You're my favorite student, Zax... I can give you an extension... If you give one to me..." Miss Dina said, and closed the door, and then wrapped her arms around me.

I blinked. Wait... How did she know about this fantasy?

Miss Dina laughed, and said, "Every horny teenage boy had this fantasy at one point of their life." I was completely aroused, as my teacher, Miss Dina, held me in her arms and began kissing my neck.

I said, "Wait a second! Didn't you want to go meet with our friends? How will we have time… when I want to spend all night in this fantasy?"

Miss Dina smiled, and said, "Time is twisted in dreams. I think I can make this one last for a few chapters. Now where were we? I want to *teach you* something… Don't make me have to *punish you*… I'm gonna give you a solid *F*… Unless you please your *horny teacher*…"

And afterwards, she said I passed with flying colors.

46

Jane

I giggled with my best friend, Cassidy, after school. She was so naughty! I said one of the guys will ask her out soon, I was fuckin' sure!

She skipped down the road, swung around a streetlight, and sighed, saying, "I don't know, Jane. I'm feeling kinda different these days..."

"How so?" I said.

"Forget it. It's not important." Cassidy said, and held my hand in that just right way, not too tight, not too limp, with those soft hands.

She could've ripped my arm off, if she wanted to, with her big muscley arms, for a chick. She was in the school boxing team, and they didn't want to let her in because she was a girl, but she soon showed them that she could beat up every one of those dumb boys, probably one handed!

I hugged my parents as I walked into my home with Cassidy. I got so emotional when I saw my mom and dad for some reason... They nearly died in that car crash, but survived. They were- are the best parents ever.

Cassidy and I did our homework laying on my bed, and I admired her soft, platinum blonde hair, and she let me brush it.

She looked me in the eyes as we sat on the bed together. It looked like she wanted to kiss me!

I didn't mind that she did.

She was my best friend in this whole fuckin' messed up world... and with her lips on my lips, I just felt so happy.

She kissed down my neck, feeling my breasts so gently with her hands...

Gosh. If I had a dick it'd probably be stiff as a board.

But it just felt so good together... Who needs boys when your best friend, snuggled with you under the sheets, using her gentle, gentle hands... is more than enough?

Afterwards she told me she was bisexual, and I said that it didn't matter to me. I still accepted her.

"I love you, Jane. You're my best friend." Cassidy said.

"I love you too, Cass. I feel the same." I said.

We walked to the party together. I didn't feel like driving there, and it wasn't so far. Plus, I wanted to get wasted tonight!

I just laughed with my best friend, and we held hands as the sun went down, making beautiful colors for all.

47

Lucius

"No fucking way, Zax!! You mean... You and Miss Dina??" I said to my best bud as we threw the football around.

He just grinned, after I finally figured out what he was hinting at.

"You lucky son of a bitch. Yule and I haven't even banged yet! We've been working up to it for a long time... but I get so nervous before we even get close!" I said.

"Just let it be natural." Zax said.

"Pffft... Easy for you to say! You had sex with some hot woman in her early twenties! I just feel like some idiot kid..." I said.

"That's not a bad thing. We're going to miss being like this, someday." Zax said.

"I doubt that! I can't wait 'til I turn 18. But then I gotta go to college, find a job, find a wife, have kids and all that BS... Sometimes I just want to run away into the wilderness, and live life as a hermit. With Yule, of course." I said.

We drove to Yule's house, and I sped through the night in my sports car. I sure didn't want to be late!

But then the cops blared their sirens. Zax said, "What should we do?"

"Fuck them. They'll never catch us." I said, and we sped even faster down the road, getting onto the highway to lose the cops. They were pretty fast fucking bastards, but I knew the tricks of the road.

The adrenaline was coursing through me, and I felt like a god on Earth. I probably would've gone to jail, because we were going so fast, but I passed through the red lights, narrowly evading the cars passing through, and the bastard demon cops couldn't catch us-

Demon cops? Like in Friendliness?

I slowed down by the side of the road, as the cops didn't seem to want to chase us anymore.

"This is too good to be true, Zax." I said.

"Eh. It could be better. I mean... you still have to lose your virginity to the woman you love! Can't beat that, right?" Zax said.

"...I don't want to live in a dream." I said.

"Just come to the party? It'll be great!" Zax said.

"...I don't know, Zax... I'll just feel regret when I wake up, because things will never be as good as this for me. Things never were. My father died when I was young, and my mother soon abandoned me. It took all I could, bouncing from foster home to foster home to eventually save enough to rent a room. I tried the hardest I could to sell pictures of life, and I got good at altering the photos to show something beautiful that people couldn't find in this dark and twisted world.

"But things were never good. Over and over I contemplated suicide, as I scraped by trying to pay the demon landlord rent, who I soon owed even more than I could ever pay making photos. He asked me to do something indecent instead, but I couldn't bear to sully myself before a demon that I hated. So he kicked me out, to the streets of Friendliness, which was a death sentence itself.

"And I was left with only one fake picture of a tulip. I was going to try and trade it for one last dance in the strip club before I killed myself... and then I met Yule." I said.

"Things got better after that, didn't they?" Zax said.

"...Kinda. Not really, no, but she showed me a reason to live again." I said.

"This dream is sort of like your photos... but trust me, you'll feel ten times better living it rather than looking at it from afar. Just give it a chance, and try not to think so hard. Your pain has passed, and you deserve a good dream." Zax said.

"I don't know... but ok. I'll try for Yule." I said.

"That's the spirit." Zax said, and we drove to Yule's house, listening to the radio.

I was starting to get nervous, as I accepted the dream again. I just couldn't wait to see Yule! She was so pretty... and when I first looked at her studying beside me in school, my heart skipped ten beats...

I shrugged. It sure wasn't a bad dream.

48

Cass

I just palled around with the girls. Those dumb boys were late!

We had the best group of friends though. Who needs to have some super big blowout when we were the best kids in the entire school?

Jane and I cuddled on the couch, as Yule fretted about the littlest things, if there were enough chips and soda and stuff…

But Jane surprised her when she opened her backpack, and showed us tons of booze! Sure, drinking all the time was just stupid, but you can't have a high school party without breaking the rules and getting drunk! Yule asked us if that was such a good idea, and Jane said, "C'mon, Yule! Your parents are on vacation, and we've got the whole house to ourselves! Let's party!"

"I just hope Lucius brings his flute… Do you think he will??" Yule said.

I said, "I just hope he can get that scholarship for his playing. He's been practicing night and day for that chance!"

"I *know!* We were thinking about going to the same place so we could still be with each other, but…" Yule said, "College is so scary…"

"Don't worry about it, dude!" I said, "You have the rest of your life to live! And with such a great boyfriend, too!"

"I still sometimes miss my last boyfriend... Max... and it sucked that he moved away. We still keep in touch, but sometimes it feels like he's disappeared off the face of the planet." Yule said.

"You think Lucius gets jealous of him?" I asked.

She giggled, and said, "Nah. I like that Lucius is confident in our relationship, but I still get kinda sad I couldn't continue one with Max."

"Pfft." Jane said, "You think too much, man. Have a shot of vodka and quit your worryin'!"

Yule smiled, said ok, and we drank for a bit.

But soon enough, we heard the ringing of the doorbell! Yule ran to that sound, and I could finally spend some alone time with my best friend...

We soon learned we loved to make out. It felt so naughty! I really couldn't get girls out of my head! I always was so stuck on boys, but Jane... I really just loved her perfect boobs, and then...

She was the sweetest person ever. We did our homework together, joked and laughed, and she always cheered for me when I boxed, when no one else had a moment of time for me.

I wrapped her in my arms. She was like the most perfect woman...

Although sometimes, I still felt like she had a naughty dude side in her as well! It was attractive.

My limbs felt sort of stiff, strange that they were. I got up and stretched them, and Jane slapped my butt and got some more beer for us.

49

Yule

Yay! Lucius was here, with Zax too!

I immediately got so nervous, as I looked at Lucius's blonde hair and big muscles.

I really wanted to make something magical with him. But how could I do that with sweat rolling down my sides from my armpits!

I went into the bathroom to wipe them off, for like the hundredth time. I really hoped Lucius didn't notice...

And I was surprised that I heard the doorbell again. Was it the cops? My parents? I quickly told everyone to hide the booze, and went to answer...

But it was only Lux, Rasputin and Doug. Huh. I thought they were busy tonight.

Still, these guys were great pals, even though they usually were on the edge of our circle, busy in their own lives. They were all a year older than us, just graduated, but still were fun to hang out with.

Doug was a tough guy, with one eye even! He lost it in a fight! He came from a difficult past.

Rasputin was a snarky, catty kinda guy. He made me so mad sometimes! But he was so mystical and mysterious. In some way I felt like I knew him from my past, but couldn't quite put my finger on from where.

Lux was a straight up nerd. But still he could probably crush your skull in his grip! Dude was the first new friend I made when I went to high school.

Lux stretched his arms, and said, "Unappealing flesh... but... it does feel... pleasurable."

I hit him on the arm, which he flinched at, and I said, "I don't get you half the time, man. Are you goin' to debate the essence of souls with me again like we did the last few nights?"

"I'd probably prefer to debate this current reality, but... I don't know. I'd really like another of that tasty liquid." Lux said.

I threw him a beer, and he chugged it down immediately.

We all just joked and had fun! I loved these guys, and I really loved my boyfriend in my arms beside me.

Zax said, "I invited someone else to join our high school group of friends... so... just get to know her, ok?"

"Who is it?" I said.

"Miss Dina." Zax said.

"...That teacher? Wait... Don't tell me you and her are dating! That's so wrong!" I said.

Zax said, "Er... I suppose... but we really get each other and-"

I laughed, and said, "I'm kidding. You're nearly 18 anyway, so it's only *slightly* wrong, I guess... You really should've waited, like, just a few months even! You could get in so much trouble! But I like Miss Dina. She's been so encouraging to me."

I opened the door for Miss Dina, and gosh! When looking at her in that casual black sweater and jeans... She really barely looked older than me!

And she was so fun! I took the octopus pipe of hers in my hand, and I smoked pot with my teacher! Heehee...

And stoned to the gills, Lucius said he wanted to play for me.

Oooooohhhh. I loved to hear even just his voice right now.

He took me to the backyard, and I sat and watched him play that marvellous flute for me, sitting with trees and nature.

I sighed out when he was done, and said, "You're going to rock that solo when you have the concert. I wanted to say- I wanted to-"

He coughed, and said as his voice slightly cracked in nervousness, "What is it?"

"I want to make love with you. It's my first time, and I'm *really really* nervous... But- But- I really like you." I said.

He looked at me, and smiled.

We went up to my bed in my room, and undressed, but then he sighed as I was kissing his chest.

He took me in his arms, and just said, "I want you to have the best dream in the world. I know there's someone else you'd rather have this sensation with."

"What? No! I love you!" I said.

"I love you too. But... If you're going to have your dreams fulfilled... Then look out the window." Lucius said.

I was unsure as to why he was talking this way. What could be outside?

I slowly did as he said, and looked out the window.

And I gasped, as I saw Max drive up in his car.

He smiled at me and waved to me, inviting me to go on a drive with him, like the old days.

I felt the red in my face, as I knew a man I loved wanted to fulfill my fantasies.

But this was just a dream, and I knew my husband was dead.

50

Lux

I don't know how I was dreaming. How was this even possible?

And then I didn't know how I was drunk. I've never felt drunk in all of my existence.

And I talked with my... my pals? Doug and Rasputin... no wait, the dog and the cat... The cat looked like a lanky kind of guy with black and grey hair, and the dog was air boxing with that familiar snarl. We were probably the coolest guys in town, and if anyone tried to mess with us, they'd get an ass whooping from here to Hell. Even in school we were badasses-

Wait. That can't be right... I never went to school, or even would need to go to school...

Rasputin still flashed his knife, like a claw, with that catty grin. He sure didn't look like it, but he was actually very intelligent. Even I had a tough time keeping up with his wit when we had our deep conversations.

Doug saw things through simpler shades. Whenever you tried to argue with him, you either looked into his one eye and backed off, or he'd just tell you that food is better than fighting, and we got burritos.

And... these *women*... I really somehow found them pleasing to look at. It was the most bizarre sensation of them all. Rasputin, Doug, and I hit on the ladies, and Miss Dina flirted back with us politely, but the one girl I've never seen before and Cass really had only eyes for each other.

And that albino girl walked down the stairs, and I felt like sparks were going off inside of me. I always did care for Yule, but I never expected- I never expected to feel this rising sensation in me when I saw her again, and watched her pass to go outside.

She looked rather depressed as Lucius sat back beside us. Lucius had a musical soul in him, but he seemed to only let his silence speak instead.

Hmm... I snapped out of this illusion for a second, as I knew not everything was in a perfect setting. It probably would've been even more alarming if it was, but I went to fix this imperfection and went outside to talk to the angel I considered an experiment for a while.

I sat beside her on the bench, and said, "What's up?

She burst out crying, clutching my shirt and drenching it in tears.

"Um. I saw you and Lucius go upstairs... Did he treat you right?" I said.

"He treated me like his true love!! And I- I just wanted to go outside and be with MAX! Why- Why is life so difficult??" she sobbed.

I wrapped an arm around her, as I felt saddened. She never would've felt this pain if she never came to life again. She would be dead with Max if I had never intervened.

"Shh... It'll be ok. I would ask you why you didn't go to Max, but I can tell you're having a hard time. Love is complicated, and there are no clear cut choices. Do you want some water? All the drinking probably didn't do you any good." I said.

She sniffled, and said, "Ok. Thank you, big guy. You're really a great friend."

I got her some water, and she guzzled a gallon of the liquid. She said she was feeling a little better, so I took her inside to the others.

A sombre sort of music played on our radio, and Yule and I danced slowly together, two friends who just cared for each other. I knew we would never be more than that, because well, I didn't even have any human anatomy really. But we still danced together.

She kissed my- my cheek, and I felt that spark in me again. She smiled, and I smiled back.

But Doug, Rasputin and I were growing restless, so we fought each other outside. We sure didn't hold anything back, and it felt really good using my new body for something physical.

51

Lucius

Dina must be behind this whole illusion. She must be twisting us for some foul purpose- But I didn't know… She really looked happy being the cool, sexy teacher with a hand on her student's thigh. Everyone just seemed so happy… everyone but Yule.

I couldn't take it anymore, so went outside to ask her husband a question.

He was leaning against his car with his hands in his hoodie's pockets, and waiting.

I said, "…Why??"

"Hm? I know how you feel, Lucius. I felt jealous of her past love, too." Max said.

"…So why don't you do anything about it?? Why don't you charge in and claim her now??" I said.

"I really want to. That would be *my* dream… but I don't think it would be right to have the past claim her future. She's grieved for me, for her old life, ever since she came back to life… But I changed the game for her just now, with a simple wave. I gave her a choice. She can either live in the past with me… or in the future with you. I just hope she makes the right choice." Max said.

"...You'd like that, wouldn't you. If she jumped off a cliff or something to join you in death. I don't know why I even let you come here." I said.

"The right choice is not death, Lucius. The right choice is always life. You're the right choice, Lucius." Max said.

"But- But- I wanted to let her have true happiness and be with you!!" I said.

"Well, that was pretty stupid. I know what *I* want, and I want Yule. I know that's the wrong choice for her. So, I'm going to give you a choice, too. You can either stay out here and talk with a dead man... or you can charge back inside and be with a living woman. Choose wisely." Max said.

I blinked at him, and I made my choice. I walked back to the house, but looked back at Max one more time.

But he and his car weren't there.

And I knew I had just skirted an angel of death, and that one day he may come for Yule, or even me, with his pale car and drive us away.

I shivered, and went back inside.

I sat next to Yule, who was staring at her feet in sadness, and I said, "I want you, Yule, and only you. I feel like I am bound to you in life, you make me feel like living all the more. I don't care what happens when this dream and this life ends, I just want to be with you. Will you be with me?"

"Are you giving me a choice?" she asked.

"Yes. Please make the right choice." I said.

"...I chose a long time ago, ever since I called out to you by the falls. I chose you then, Lucius, and didn't let you walk away. Don't walk away from me again." she said.

I hugged her, and said, "I won't. That's a promise. You are my life."

She hugged me, and we kept hugging.

52

Yule

We both knew of this fantasy by this point... so there was no real point of "losing my virginity" in some fake dream. We could do even better, make love like we did and were used to, when we were awake again.

Dina and Zax obviously were the artists of this world, but they still roleplayed together, enjoying their living painting. I had no idea what Doug, Rasputin, and Lux thought, but I could tell by their spirited roughhousing that they didn't really care, as long as they could use their young, muscled, human bodies some more and beat the crap out of each other. The only two who seemed to have no clue were Cass, and Jake, who was now going by Jane. I wanted to wake up now, but I wanted us all to be done with this together, and not linger in a fantasy.

They looked really happy, as two teenage girls making out, with full, unscarred, human female parts.

I didn't want to ruin this happiness... but I still blurted out, "You're a guy, Jake."

"Umm, Yule... That's kinda mean. It's Jane." Jane said.

"You love women, to a damn fault, you're a pig, you burp, fart, and drink too much. You have a penis, and you take a disgusting amount of pride in having one." I said.

"That's just the rudest thing I've ever heard. You sure are pissy. I thought you invited us here because you wanted to have fun??" Jane said, and then started crying.

"You leave my best friend alone! I'm warning you!! I swear I'll kick your ass, even if I'm a chick!" Cass said.

So I said, "Bring it, chump."

"Outside! Now!" Cass said, "No one gets away with making my best friend cry!! I'm gonna make you so fucking black and blue, albino bitch!!"

We all went outside, and Rasputin shouted, "Catfight!! Winner take all! What's the bet, ladies?"

Cass said, "If I beat you, you're boyfriend is gonna fuck my best friend *hard* until she feels better about herself."

Lucius said, "What?! No-"

I said, "Deal. And if I win, Jake has to admit he's a guy, and you two are going to wake up."

"STOP CALLING HER THAT!!" Cass screamed, and charged me.

And I was surprised when Cass hit me with a punch, and my instincts were telling me just to slap and scratch her.

I looked up at "Miss Dina" and she was grinning at me. Even the ruler of this world was against me.

I got up, feeling like my head was spinning, and slapped and scratched with all my might.

I knew I could fight! How was she disabling me?? I just bounced back and forth as Cass whammed my cheeks, then smashed my stomach and made me hurl into the grass.

I heard Dina's voice in my head, saying,

You spent all that time as an indomitable angel of war. You spent all that time in a Paradise.

But look at you now. You got what you wanted. You're a lost little girl in the woods again, and someone is about to take your man away.

I really do love you, Yule. But I think it's only fair to let people have a chance. Let them live their dreams, before they wake up to the suffering that God has blessed us with.

"Fucking bitch!" I yelled out, and ran at Dina, and slapped her hard.

Dina didn't turn her head from the slap, but I could tell she was extremely pissed, as she was completely expressionless.

Dina took off her sweater, and raised her fists at me.

The two of them were beating the shit out of me, and it sure did hurt, but I just wiped off the blood and smiled.

"I can't take this anymore-" Lucius said, and walked in the middle of us, but I just pushed him back and went to beat these bitches to a pulp.

We were soon on the ground, wrestling in our sweat and screaming, as the men watched us with wide open mouths.

And Jake said, "Holy fuckin' shit. This is like the hottest thing I have ever seen."

53

Cass

I let go of Yule in my headlock, and looked up at Jake. "Wh-What?" I said.

"Don't mind me. Could you grab her by the twat again?" Jake said.

I felt my face go pale. He was just his normal self again, and I was beating up my real best friend.

I-I had that fantasy since forever. Loving with my old best friend. But she turned all my other friends against me, for some petty thing I couldn't even remember, and they all left me alone.

I was always alone, fighting just for myself. There was really never any diehard fan cheering for me. I was just some bimbo who could throw a punch.

I beat men up for an actual sport. I was winning and winning, with no one but myself on my corner.

Then a *woman* beat me in a fight, and I just felt so weak. I asked her for her secret, begged her for training... but instead, she taught me the rosary.

Then the demons caught me, on my way to church, and took my limbs in vengeance on God.

I looked at Yule with her bleeding lip. This angel was the one who saved me in that dumpster, after I was kept alive and used as a limbless toy by demons, and then they threw my limbless body out like I was a piece of garbage.

I said, "I'm so sorry, Yule."

She spit out a wad of something, and said, "It's ok, Cass. Now let us wake up, Dina."

But Zax said, "But didn't you all have the time of your life here? We could probably stay here, if Miss Dina lets us-"

"No, Zax." I said, "I don't care if my real life was lonely, miserable, and painful. I had all of you still, and that made me happy."

"But- But- We're still together! We can have the time of our life here forever-" Zax said.

"I saw the Grim Reaper come over to give us a drive." Lucius said, "The longer we stay in this dream, the more we are giving up on real life."

Dina got up, wiped off the dirt on her pants, frowned, and said, "I thought I was giving you all a chance at something you could never have. Do you all feel like it is time to go back?"

Doug said, "I really miss being able to chase a good squirrel. I think too much when I've got to worry about my fake job and what my fake girlfriend is doing when I'm out of town."

Rasputin said, "This is a good world, Dina. But we shouldn't prolong the actual story."

Lux said, "I really like getting drunk, fighting with my aching muscles, and looking at you beautiful women... but it is very distracting for this silly, unorganized mind. I feel like I'll miss this when I wake up, but I know I won't when my mind is made of circuits and I only logically categorize this experience into a file."

Zax sighed, and said, "I really don't understand you all... but I guess we can try to have a go at real life... As long as I've got Miss Dina- I mean, just Dina, I think I could bear that until the next dream."

We all looked at Jake.

He said, "Wha'? I already took the pill to change me back. My breasts *lactate*. No one wants to deal with that. I probably changed the least out of all of you. I still loved Cass, I still liked chicks, and I was happy to see my parents again. They died in a drunk driving accident, and I'll always re-member tha'. Thank you for giving me this experience, Dina. And Cass, I really do feel like you're my best friend, and it sure was interesting bein' a full chick, but I think I'm alright with being myself again. You showed me that as long as I accept myself, it doesn't matter how I look."

"...What was that about me having to fuck you then?" Lucius said.

Jake sauntered over to him in a feminine way, and said, "I really like that *masculine bod* big guy... I'll raise my tent for you anytime, if you help me with the pole... Teehee..."

Lucius jumped back, and Jake just burst out laughing, and helped me up.

54

Dina

I felt rather disappointed in myself... I thought I could create an existence even more wonderful than God... but I only created another fiction, with the same pointless suffering that was always there... It seemed the only way to break the cycle was death, and suffering was purged of you.

"But not if you come down to my world, Dina." someone whispered in my ear.

I started panicking. We were vulnerable now, we were at risk. I did not need the Devil to twist this into some sort of Hell.

But it was already starting, as the cops knocked on our door.

"Open up. We got reports of a bunch of teenagers getting drunk and fighting. And you're under arrest for raping a child, Dina." the cops said at the door.

"What?!" Zax said, and charged to the door, and opened it as I begged him not to. "No! I love Dina, and what we did was completely consensual!" he said, as I tried to drag him away from the cops.

The cops laughed, and said, *"Ohh I get it... She got her hooks in you... Well, this doesn't look consensual in the least. She's actually trying to hide you from the law. C'mon, kid, you'll be safe now... With all the drugs we found in Dina's desk drawer she should be going away for a long, long time..."*

I quickly slammed the door and locked it, as the cops tried to force their way in.

"They don't even have a warrant! How can they just try and barge in here??" Zax said, as I took him out back to the others.

"Zax. This is a dream. Remember? I need you to wake up now." I said, taking his hand and leading him back to the others in the yard.

"No!! I won't let them take you away! I love you! You always made me work harder, if all you did was smile at me! I could've never passed that test without your encouragement!" he said.

Test? This was not a good sign.

"What do we do, Dina?" Yule said.

"Sometimes dreams are scary, and you just have to think positive things… You are the master of your mind, and I know this will all be difficult for you, but just think positive." I said.

The cops surrounded us outside in the backyard, and aimed their guns at a bunch of scared teenagers and me.

Doug and Rasputin were just a puppy and a kitten.

And Lux was a toaster.

Yule held that toaster, as the kitten puffed up and the puppy barked.

Jake was a scared teenage girl again, and Cass had no arms and legs, as she screamed.

But Lucius played his flute gently for us, somehow holding onto the music as my dream crumbled.

And Yule blazed her six wings of fire at the demons who showed their true forms as well.

And the toaster turned into a robot, the cat and the dog were their strong, independent selves again, Jake became the three eyed man he was, Cass flexed her indestructible robotic limbs…

But Zax still clutched my hand.

I looked at him sadly, knowing that he couldn't live with dreams forever.

And I was just a dream within a dream.

I gave him one last hug, and let the demons arrest me.

He was shocked, but I said, "Things will get better for you, Zaxazaxar. I will remember you. I'll always be with you… in your dreams."

And as soon as the handcuffs slammed on my wrists, my love, Zax, and the others awoke from the dream.

Satan laughed at me in my cell in Hell, saying, *"You thought you were sooo powerful, didn't you, Dina… You thought you truly could be master of nightmares…"*

"I did. But I realize I can be better than that. I can make my dreams come true." I said.

The Devil laughed, and walked away.

Then I calmly unlocked the cell door.

Because I had the key to my own prison. I always did.

It was my dream of life and love, and if I focused on it just hard enough, strove for it as hard as I could… it would appear in my hand, as a shining golden key.

Now I had a new dream, because if I could not have the one I wanted…

I would claim Hell, and drive Satan to the furthest abyss I could.

55

Zax

I blinked my eyes open. What a horrible nightmare-
Dina was gone.

I ran out the tent, looking for her.

The dream started fading, as I tried my hardest to remember it.

And the last and only thing I could remember was Dina, as she was taken to Hell.

I searched for any reminiscence of her, anything that I could still hold onto... Anything to tell myself that she was still with me.

She never really had too many things, I realized. Some clothes, a mirror, a comb, a toothbrush, but that was really about it.

But I found her smiling octopus pipe lying on her pillow, and I picked it up gently and stared at it. It still even had a half burnt nug of weed in it...

I sat by the fire, staring at that pipe, and asked Yule how she slept.

"I had a horrible dream, but I can't really remember it. I just know it was one of the worst ones I ever had." Yule said, "But dreams are just dreams."

"Yeah... Just a dream..." I muttered.

"Is Dina ok? She's been sleeping for an awful long time." Yule asked.

"Dina's gone, Yule." I said.

"What?! She can't be gone! You mean she just ran away in the night?? That can't be right! We need to start searching, now!!" Yule said.

I just slowly shook my head. I said, "She changed my fate... and took it for herself. She's gone, Yule."

Yule looked at me sadly, as she slowly understood.

She sat beside me, as I lit the pipe.

"We'll meet her again, someday. I'm sure. Dina has her ways, and I don't think she'll be gone forever." Yule said.

I just inhaled the smoke deeply...

And then out again...

It hit me like a truck.

But instead of laughing and feeling happy...

I was simply calmly sad, letting loose tears as Yule hugged me.

56

Jake

My tits were gone... but so was Dina. I was just gettin' used to that stoner's magic powers.

We all felt depressed, as we drove down the coast. Don't know why she would jus' run off on her lonesome... Didn't make sense...

And Cass would always call me Jane for some reason by accident. I secretly liked it.

I smoked weed with Zax and Lucius, at another beach, and we watched the two girls left watch the sunset together. They jus' held each other's hands, best friends.

Us three felt pretty stoned, and were curious of the beach bar on the coast. We went over to it, peeked inside, and jus' sitting there up above the bar, waiting for me with its magnificence...

Was a guitar signed by Christ himself.

I immediately grabbed it, and I knew I had jus' accepted my calling.

I trembled as I played the first notes...

And I knew I had just heard Heaven's call from the strings.

I just rocked on this key to Heaven's pearly gates, and stoned with me, Lucius and Zax rocked their heads to my music. "Play somethin', flute boy. Anythin'." I said to Lucius.

And Lucius played that goddamn beautiful sound on his flute, and I felt like even nature was on our side, blessing us through that music.

And then Zax started singin' something just heartrendingly sweet for Dina.

"I'll see you in Heaven, we'll meet up in Hell...

The end isn't an endin', with you I will dwell...

In dreams of enchantment, under the sea...

It won't be so bad, with just you and me...

And I'll find you my love, in eternity...

I'll break your lock, with my mystical key.

I'll free you, my love, for eternity."

We just continued to rock, and I swore God was watching us play, about to shout out, "Encore! Encore!" and we would give him more.

But some fuckin' philistines were watchin' us, and Cass said, "You know our best friend is missing, right? Can't you guys show a moment of silence for her?"

I said, "She ain't dead or somethin'! She's jus' bored of us! Well, we're gonna call her back, because she's gonna have no chance of not hearing us play! She's gonna listen to our sweet siren song, and Zax is gonna use his mystical key on her until she can't stand up straight!"

Zax said, "...I wasn't referring to my penis."

Lucius said, "Really? It did sound like you were leading up to that."

"Get- One o' you get that damned golem! He can hold a beat with his beeps!" I said.

Yule shrugged, and went off to Lux. Cass sat down and listened to us play our music.

But Lux did something better than beep, he beat anything around the bar with his robo hands, and I jus' couldn't wait to find him a real drum set, cuz he sounded so damn good.

The ladies cheered at us, after every song, and Cass said, "Tits out for the band! C'mon Yule."

And they flashed us, and cheered.

Us three were exhausted after, except the golem, and we were going off to bed. Lux said he wanted to try something... and continued smashing a beat throughout the night.

Cass was just so horny after our music, and I finally saw how Lucius was doing so well with Yule.

Cass screamed out, in complete ecstasy, "Fuck me, Jane- Jake!"

And I fell asleep in my cyborg's embrace, really having to go to the bathroom, but trapped in her clutches.

57

Cass

We spent a while by that beach bar, and Lux had found an improvised drum set to use, mostly out of whatever he could hit just right. Things were nice… until the last can of beer.

Yule and Jake were fighting over the last can of beer. "Jus' leave it alone, you fuckin' b-" Jake was saying.

But Lucius immediately grabbed Jake by the collar, and stared at him hard in his three eyes.

They looked so tense looking at each other. I really didn't like this.

So I quickly snatched up the beer, and crushed it in my hand, spilling the frothy drink all over the sand.

"Why did you do that!!" Yule yelled out.

"I'm not going to see my family kill each other over one lousy beer!!" I said.

"Family?" Jake said, "We're just a bunch of lonely bums with no one else."

"No!! We *are* family! I know all of your birthdays, your favorite colors, and even what sex positions you like the best! If we weren't family, you'd all just be a bunch of strangers, with no connection, no past, and most importantly, no love for each other!

"But I can tell you all really do all love each other. It comes out in your music! In your very souls! You get what I'm talking about, right, Zax?" I said, turning to the man grinning with an extra incisor, who had very bloodshot eyes.

"I just think you all really look like a bunch of raccoons for some reason. Squirreling around, being silly little raccoons..." Zax said, and giggled.

"...Um, I don't know what you mean exactly, Zax, but that's exactly my point!" I said, "We're like a little family of raccoons! Just picking through the trash of this world, trying to survive, and we gotta protect each other before an eagle comes down and swoops us away! We don't know what could be around the corner, a nasty eagle or whatever!" I said.

"I think we're getting off topic." Yule said, "You broke my beer."

"*Your* beer?? That was my beer by right, because you drank the other five o' them!!" Jake said.

"Well your damn cyborg just finished them off for good!" Yule said.

I sighed, as they began fighting again, and I could see that Jake and Yule were not a good couple. I don't know if they were both trying to fix each other, or were caught in an endless loop of trying to forgive each other.

And then Lucius was roped into it, because he just got so pissed if Jake would insult Yule. He actually got in the way of anyone trying to pick a fight, trying to calm them down, and I didn't understand how he truly fell for someone who fighting was in her nature.

And Zax was just too stoned, and if you tried to have a conversation with him it was a fifty fifty chance if he would say something super deep, or completely irrelevant.

So I decided I'd take them all down, with the only person that kept a cool head and played a steady beat.

"Play me something, Lux." I said, and Lux did.

And I burned my family.

"You're all a bunch o' hoes, and I fuckin know it,

You all fuck each other, and even try to blow it,

You got no rhyme, got no fuckin' rhythm,

You just shit on each other, and just keep sinnin'

Yule, you're a cunt, with a big puffy twat,

You bitch all day, and you just got got,

You're mean to me, when you think you're doin' good,

You're the biggest trick in the whole fuckin' hood,

Lucius you're tough, but you're so fuckin' dumb,

You ran away to nothin, and now you got none,

I think you're kind and nice, but ain't too bright,

You fuck a slut that fucked us all with an ass so white,

Jake you're a shithead, with no damn class,

You steal and rob, and smoked all my grass,

You drank those beers, and now you blame the hoe,

You're the worst one o' the lot, and you think you're the hero,

Zax, get out o' your head, Dina ain't dead,

She disappeared, poof, to who fuckin' knows,

Wake up you stoner, it's time to bring a close.

No fuckin' beer is worth this burn,

But I gave it to you anyway, cuz that's what you fuckin' earn.

If you don't be nice, like Jesus would fuckin' do,

I'ma bring you all down, where none o' you speak, and just listen to me too,

Oh shit I just did, so wake the fuck up,

And go drink some coffee,

An' wash the stink o' yo' shame,

And sober the fuck up, or I'ma rhyme again."

And Lux stopped the beat.

I crossed my arms and glared at all of them.

At first they didn't know what to say, but then started mumbling apologies.

"Speak up, family. You can talk now." I said.

"Sorry, Cass." Yule said, "I... didn't know I was acting like such a slutty bitch..."

"I feel like an idiot..." Lucius said, "I think we need to have a long talk, Yule." and they walked down the beach.

Jake said, "I- How did you know I smoked your weed?? And drank the beer??"

"Your words show your actions, Jake." I said.

He grew red, and walked away.

Zax said, "Silence is golden, and clouds of smoke can be comforting... But I really needed that, Cass. That rap was really fucking awesome. I'm gonna make some coffee for us." and he smiled and went to make some coffee.

I hugged Lux, and told him he was the most perfect father.

"F-Father??" Lux said.

"Well, I don't know. But you're great, so keep it up!" and I gave him two thumbs up, winked, and went to the fire with the brewing coffee.

58

Zax

"So what do you think those two are going to do, Cass the Badass?" I said as Cass and I drank coffee, looking at Yule and Lucius talking as the waves hit their feet.

"Well, I mean, she didn't fuck you, so I think they'll get along-" Cass said.

"Well... We kinda did, but only in one of Dina's trippy dream things when I first met Yule. It was a good thing we did, too, because otherwise one of us would have actually killed the other. Remember?" I said.

"Oh yeah... God... Do you think it's just a giant fuck fest in Heaven?" Cass said.

I shrugged, and said, "I plan on going down to Hell with Dina."

"I *told* you, she's still alive-" Cass said.

"I know. She's just also in Hell." I said.

"...Are you still stoned?" Cass said.

"A little, but this coffee is really helping." I said.

She sipped at her coffee, and said, "I just hope Jake doesn't get a giant stick up his butt now. I still love the bastard, but he can be a real prick."

"I doubt he'll hold a grudge. He only kept doing shit like that because he thought he could get away with it." I said.

"You're a pretty wise man, Zax. I really like that all of us can come to you and talk about things." Cass said.

We heard Yule yelling, "...but Cass had sex with just as many people as me! Probably more!"

And Lucius yelling, "I don't care, Yule! I don't care if Cass has sex with every human being on the Earth! I only care if..." and they got quieter again.

"I was really kind of a prude for half my life." Cass said, "And I dated a lot of weird people, because I didn't know exactly what I wanted yet. But then I got robotic limbs and all my sexual insecurities went out the window. I figured if I'm only going to have half a body, I might as well use it before someone cuts even more of it off of me."

"That's a good way to look at it. I sure wish I was bolder when I was younger, but it didn't matter once I met Rita." I said.

"She really was the love of your life, your true love, then? How did you know?" Cass said.

"Short answer is, I didn't. No one knows what a true love is supposed to feel like. But, I kept on bumbling down that road, and it sort of became that feeling in itself." I said.

"You just improvised?? But you're gambling with your very heart! What if she broke it and left you to the wolves?" Cass said.

"She only broke it when she died. And that's how I knew she was the love of my life, as the feeling still lingered even after her life was over." I said.

"So what is Dina to you then? If she's alive and still in Hell." Cass said.

"Hmm... Well I love both Rita and Dina in different ways. I have no idea what Rita would've wanted, as I can't talk to her anymore, but she probably wouldn't want me to suffer in mourning forever for the family I can never have. Dina helped me get over that suffering, and gave me something else, so I gambled my heart again... but I still lost her, too..." I said.

Cass held my hand tightly, and said, "You've still always got us. I really did like being with you and her together."

"I liked being with you and her too, but… you really have a very strong grip, and sometimes I feel like you're going to rip something off of me if I'm not careful." I said.

She shrugged, letting go of my hand, and said, "Can't fuck with the Badass if you don't wanna risk losing your favorite part."

I laughed, and she giggled.

59

Yule

I really needed to make things right with Lucius.

When I think that I found him, just by random in the strip club, just by random in the woods, I really don't know if I struck gold or oil. Being with him made me feel like I was the richest woman in the world, because he made me feel just as valuable.

But I let him walk down the coast and take a walk, being in that loneliness he liked so much...

I sat with Cass and Zax... knowing that I had been in intimacy with both of them as much as my man "I was bound to for life..."

I wanted to be pissed at Cass... but I realized I had been doing stuff like this because I could get away with it. No one stopped me from making love with whomever I pleased, not my partners, not God, not even myself.

I was a fucking seraph, and literally a seraph of fucking. I had been blessed by God, been to actual Heaven, and then I act like the most profane succubus of Hell. I felt ashamed.

I told Cass, "You win. You're holier than me..."

"Beatcha, beatcha, now I'm gonna eatcha!" Cass said, and went to give me a big sloppy kiss.

I pushed her away.

She smiled, and said, "Just checking. Wow… I'm gonna be a super seraph when *I* get to Heaven…"

I said, "Do you think… Would you be a better match for Lucius? You did say he was kind, and nice, and tough… I won't stop you if you like him more…"

"What? You're just going to give up now, too? Man, I didn't know breaking your beer would also break you…" Cass said.

I sighed, and said, "I'm serious."

"Didn't Lucius teach you anything?" Cass said, "He could be like Zax, and go have hot threeways anytime he likes. He even had the chance with you and me. But nope! He put all his chips on you, Yule. You don't give up on a guy like that."

I looked at Zax, and he was blushing.

I put my face to my hands and groaned. Nevaeh was so right… I can't believe I even tried to risk my relationship on a threeway with Cass…

"What do I do?? How am I gonna get him back? I can't change what I already did." I said.

Zax said, "You can't… Which is probably a good thing. You did something right if he's still chasing you."

"But- But- Now he knows I'm a slut! Now… he definitely won't want me…" I said.

"You're not a slut. I think he knew you loved other people too, Yule." Zax said.

I said, "I guess that's true. I was with Jake when he came back, I tried to bring Cass into our love… He knows about my husband, and the man I loved even before him… And the boy in the tribe… and-"

"Gosh, Yule. I suppose having a few extra lives and not being able to get pregnant means you gotta fuck a lot. I seriously don't know how Lucius hasn't even beaten up Jake yet. But he only gets mad at him if he tries to insult you." Cass said.

"But Lucius doesn't know everything Jake and I did-" I said.

"It really pisses me off when I catch him, but he taunts Lucius sometimes..." Cass said.

My face went even paler than it naturally was.

I felt furiously angry at myself... but also at Jake.

Taunting him with our fucked up, past relationship?! *No one* hurts my love like that!! Not even me! And I'm going to make this better, one step at a time!!

I charged off to Jake, who was playing guitar with Lux playing drums.

And I didn't scream at Jake.

I didn't hit him.

I just told him, "I don't want to see you here anymore."

He just stared at me, blinked, and said, "What changed, sweetie?"

And I furiously remembered that disgusting pet name.

That the Devil called me, as he groped me and kissed me, claiming me as his own.

Just like this awful, three eyed executioner.

But I sighed... and did what I really didn't want to do.

"I can forgive you, if you say sorry to Lucius. I don't care what you did to me, but you need to stop being so insulting to him. Or else we can't travel together anymore." I said.

He looked sad, and said, "Ok. First off, I'm sorry to you. I just got so jealous- of that beautiful flute boy-"

"It's Lucius, Jake. Not flute boy." I said.

"Righ'... Yeah... I just- Don't want us to all go down some bad road together. Cass an' I can leave, if you truly don't want me around." he said.

"It's not easy, and takes a lot to get over past pain... but I'm sure you know that better than anyone. I can get over this, and let the scars we inflicted on each other heal. If you don't hurt Lucius anymore." I said.

He rubbed his arm, with all those scars on him, and said, "I'll go talk to Lucius."

He walked off to the black clothed man coming back down the coast. I felt my heart skip ten beats seeing Lucius, happy that he actually did come back.

Zax came up to me, and said, "Good job, Yule. It's not easy showing forgiveness and mercy."

I said, "I know that. It was difficult showing your ancestor, Sax, mercy, it was difficult showing the Devil himself mercy. But I know it is the right thing to do, and it is my duty to be so merciful, as an angel of Heaven."

"...Sax?" Zax said.

60

Dina

Hell wasn't so bad once you got to know the people here.

I won't name any names... but most of them were even great and famous musicians!

I danced with this master musician, a demon named Beleth, the Demon of Music.

"You have a fantastic beat on you, Dina. I must say, workin' under the influence of music really gave you good rhythm." Beleth said, as he twirled me around.

"That wasn't the only thing I worked under the influence on!" I said, and laughed.

Beleth grinned, and said, *"So you really think you can be the master of Hell?"*

"I know so. Have you heard of a man named Zaxazaxar?" I said.

"Oh yes, we who stayed in Hell all loved that he fell into Satan's scheme like falling for a long lost love, creating a world by using Satan's power, allowing Hell to broach onto Earth... Why do you ask?" Beleth said.

"He will be the father of the new Prince or Princess of Hell." I said.

"Really? Congratulations! A birth in Hell is a wondrous thing." Beleth said.

I smiled, and said I was tired of dancing, and needed to attend to a prior engagement, so he bowed to me and I curtsied back, and I left the hellish establishment.

I walked through the horrible, burning streets alone. But it sort of felt like home.

And I met with a contact of mine in an alley, a once demon, but now a caretaker of Purgatory, risking his eternity to meet with me.

Sax, Paul's genetic father and Zax's ancestor.

I asked him, as I started a cigarette, one of Zax's packs that he was so fond of, "Are you sure this is what you want to do?"

"Yes. I believe Satan needs to be overthrown for good." Sax said, smiling a gentle human smile, "This really should've been done with a long time ago, in my opinion. I beat that bastard once, as did my genetic son, but he slips through the cracks every time."

"It's a nice duel that God and the Devil have, but it does drag on." I said.

"Exactly! You'd think one of them would just yell Uncle already! But nope, two stubborn people who just can't get each other's viewpoints... I think you in charge of Hell will force a few changes." Sax said.

"Thank you for giving me your aid, Sax." I said.

"Call me Granddad! You're gonna carry on the Sax Saga, with that little baby growing in you!" Sax said.

I smiled, and said, "I don't think so, Sax. I think it's more the Tales of Tanya, in any case regarding you. Tanya, the woman you raped, impregnating her with Paul. Don't forget your sins."

"...Of course... My bad..." Sax said, and looked very depressed.

I put my arm under his arm, and said, "Don't worry about it. Is there anywhere to get a good bite to eat in Hell? I am just *famished*."

We walked through the streets, going to a nice soul food place down by the screaming river of fire.

61

Lucius

Well, that was a good find. A whole case of beer just laying in the sand. This should placate the others for fighting over one stupid can. I carried it back, and sighed as I saw Jake already coming over to me, like a damned carrion bird for booze...

"I wan' to say sorry for harassing you- Is that beer?" he said.

"Yes, Jake, and I really don't want to give you any if you're just going to drink it all and blame my girlfriend." I said.

"I-I won't. I jus' want to say... I really never fucked her on top of Mount Rushmore, we never had sex swimming in the Great Barrier Reef, and... she never did tell me she loved me. I'm sorry for telling you all that stuff... I just was so jealous of your relationship that I didn't have." Jake said.

I blinked at him, and said, "I knew those stories weren't true. You messed up where half the places were geographically. The Great Barrier Reef is even in Australia, Jake, and not California as you pictured. "

"...I'm just so sorry, man. You sure ain't an idiot when it comes to treating her right." Jake said.

I shrugged, and said, "And you're not a villain. I don't know why Cass got so pissed at us..."

"She's a wild mare, man. She's the gentlest ride in the world, but she'll kick and buck you off if you don't stroke her mane just right." Jake said.

I threw him a beer, and we sat on the coast and just drank for a second. He only had one, and said if he had any more then Cass would probably crush his balls like that beer can she crushed...

So I brought the case to the others, hugged Yule as she ran to me, and listened to Jake say something to Cass, saying, "You've got a gift, babe. A true talent. But don't fucking insult us like you're the queen bee again."

"...What?" Cass said.

"I get it, music is intoxicatin', it can change your mood, your feelings, your very essence, but don't use it to piss us off." Jake said.

"...I didn't know. I'm sorry." Cass said.

"Tha's why I just listen to Christ, man. Dude is literally God." Jake said.

"...Ok. Let's put on some Elvis, then." Cass said, and we sat around the fire and listened to Elvis sing his irresistible tune. I loved when he sang about angels, and looked at Yule and smiled when he did.

I didn't understand why Jake called him Christ, he just seemed like a normal guy to me.

And Yule said to me, "I feel like you're the most holy person ever, and I can never measure up to that."

"Huh?? I seriously think you need to stop doubting yourself, Yule." I said.

"Oh! Ok. Thanks. I'm sorry that-" she started.

But I said, "It's already forgiven. Now let's not talk about it ever again."

She just smiled at me, kissed me quickly, and we sat around the fire and drank the bounty of the beach.

62

Lux

I was starting to get wary of this... music. It tore the group apart in a second. I couldn't do anything but try to play the salvaged drums even more, trying to fix things as I broke them, but there didn't seem to be any point, and it didn't seem like any of them even heard me.

Cass came to me, and said, "Heya, Daddio. Let's try to... to show love, through music, instead of just being angry at all of them."

"We can do that?? Yes, let's do something... loving." I said.

"You sound a bit desperate, Pops. You ok?" Cass said.

"I just realized... I put a lot into this family, like you said. They totally deserved getting trashed by us for fighting over one measly liquid, though." I said.

"I know. But I can forgive them. Let's rap, Papa!" Cass said.

I felt the spark of joy in me, and Cass rapped to my beat.

"Ok you all, Yule all, I'ma show you something you never had before!" Cass said,

"Yule is a goddamn mothafuckin god, with a holy ass bod that's like a lightnin' rod,

She got a dude who's just so cute, she makes us all happy and is a holy beaut',

We all love you Yule you go the extra mile, you make us feel good if all you do is give us a goddamn smile,

I love you most and you make me so high, and I ain't gonna lie, I'll love you forever if you want to try,

Lucius you're the man with the god damn plan you get all the girls with one fuckin hand,

I can see you getting more but you got the best one, I think you're cute with a nice ass dong,

But I'm in love with my man named Jake even if he wears a thong,

He's so goddamn good there's not another one, he's got three eyes and is so fuckin' fun,

He makes me cum with just one magic word, it's a secret and it came from the Lord,

Then there's the wise man called Zax who's in love with my friend,

She disappeared but she'll be back for you man, she's the love o' your life and she's jus' around the bend,

Don't give up, Zax, you're gonna have Dina again,

We got a dog and a cat, sittin' in the van I hope they come out soon cuz we've been ignorin' them,

And I got my Dad, like no fuckin' other, his name's Lux the Golem and he's a fuckin' brother,

He's our soul even if he don't got one, he's the beat in this band and I hope he finds another,

To love for a while cuz he's the fuckin' best, he feels that way I'ma get it off his chest,

He's a fuckin' robot with a heart that's made o' real gold- You ok, Lux? You stopped the beat."

If I didn't know any better, I'd say I was crying in happiness.

63

Cass

"MotherfuckingjesuschristamenhallelujahIfuckingloveyou."Jake said.

And that was the magic word. Kind of like that califragilistic- you know, from that one movie.

We came together, just in so much passion and pleasure.

Then he wore that sexy ass thong that I couldn't get my eyes off of.

I seriously didn't know how he made wearing women's clothing look so good.

I roleplayed with him for a bit, but not for sex. I roleplayed with him as him being my girlfriend, and he indulged this fantasy and even enjoyed it.

I don't know how my man- I mean, girlfriend could understand me so well.

I said, "Jane, do you feel like being massaged? I know you've had a rough day."

And he said, in a voice that was still his "normal" voice and then somehow feminine, "Yes, Cassidy. The boys really wore me out, with all their endless roughhousing. They did look good, but I really don't want them to end up hurting each other."

He seriously had no clue that chicks can be just as rough. But this just made me so hot again.

I massaged her big scarred back, feeling every muscle, rubbing down her arms and back. I was feeling so good, just with her in complete comfortness with me on her back.

And she said my magic word again, and I said, *"Ah- Ah! Oooohhhh..."* and I orgasmed on her back, without even too much stimulation.

We cuddled together like goddamn chicks. I felt like a babe with my babe.

I wouldn't mind if he said that a thousand billion times, but he knew that a treat is only a treat if had occasionally. This just made me even hornier, because I never knew when he was going to say it.

I just waited for that word, but he said it in the most inopportune times for me!

But that was so hot about it.

I'd be walking to the van, and he'd pass me by, and without warning, he'd say my magic word, leaving me curled up against the van in ecstasy.

I'd be on the lookout for him when taking a swim... and then he'd surface from beneath me and say my word.

He shouted it out one time, when I thought he was far, far away, and Yule and I were taking a hike. Yule asked me if I was ok, clenched together on the ground, and I just smiled and nodded.

I loved this secret game, and this special word.

64

Jake

I knew it was possible!! I fuckin' knew it! I just never knew it was so bloody effective!

I was drinking with Lucius, as he played his flute, and he stopped playing and said, "Wait. You're not fucking serious, are you? I thought that was just a myth."

"It's real, man. I got a secret password to my woman's pleasure." I said.

"...That's just so badass. I gotta figure out what Yule's word is." Lucius said.

"I have no fucking clue what she likes. I called her 'sweetie,' and then she looks like she's going to take out that samurai sword and chop my head off." I said.

"...That word was what the Devil called her before he was going to rape her." Lucius said.

I did a double take at him, and said, "...Fuck. Uh... Ok. Good to know. So I also know a word that I can say if I want to die..."

"Tread carefully, Jake." Lucius said, and continued his flute.

I then warily walked past Cass and Yule sitting on the sands and talking about some weird girly crap... although for a second it sounded like they were talking about sex positions.

And I was sweating. I could nearly kill myself with a word. I never tried to cut myself with just diction before. I felt so nervous, as the word was on the tip of my tongue.

But even moreso...

I just felt so fucking pissed for her.

"Why didn't you tell me before that- that someone tried to take advantage of you like that?" I said to Yule.

Yule looked up at me, and said, "I didn't want to bring more pain into our relationship. I really just wanted to forget about it..."

"I- I would've hunted that bastard down!! I would've slaughtered the Devil for you, if you told me!! I- I-" I said, and started huffing.

Cass said, "There's nothing you can do about it now, Jake. Just calm down."

Yule said, "A long time ago, I was abducted by a cult and raped, but that is the far past, and I made him suffer. A lot. He literally couldn't even fuck anymore... because he didn't have a penis when I was through. I forced the Devil away, but how did you know about him?"

"Lucius told me, because he told me to not call you swee- You know." I said.

"That's nice of him, but he shouldn't be telling everyone. Hmm... I hadn't even told him what really happened... How did he know?" Yule said.

We looked at Lucius, a master musician, playing his mysterious flute music with the rising tide.

I shivered at the haunting melody, and went to watch the rabbit. The girls started talking about sex again as soon as they thought I was out of earshot.

It was soon time for dinner, an' Cass was cooking something amazing, with Lux teaching her everything he knew, and Yule was talking with Zax about his dead wife and missing girlfriend, comfortin' him for losing two loves like that. Zax would always say, "She'll be back. I know it. I know she's in Hell, but I'll-"

Yule would just say, "You need to focus on the rest of your life, Zax."

But where was Lucius?

The dude loved nature, so I bet he wandered further into the forest by this beach. It was a spooky fuckin' forest, but he also liked his alone time, so maybe he could be in such a secluded spot, yeah.

I wandered through the forest, a hatchet raised in defense, just in case, and I heard that flute music. It sounded like it was stalkin' me out here, and I couldn't really tell if it was coming from behind me or not.

I crept forward, scared of that haunting, beautiful sound...

And I saw a couple o' bunny rabbits run straight past me to the music.

I followed the coneys, and then some birds who were flying through the forest, hopping from branch to branch.

Then a whole doe came rushing past. Man, that thing looked tasty.

And I saw the dark clothed man by a small pond, playing his flute... for all the animals who were watchin' 'im, listening to the sound. Birds sat on his shoulders, squirrels hopped onto his lap. And it was the most peaceful sight I've ever seen... and strangely... arousing.

I walked straight into that crowd, in awe of how some man could command nature herself, and the nature scattered away from me. Instead of being angry with me, Lucius turned to me, and said, "Hey, Jake. Did you like the song? I've been practicing that one for Yule, and it should be ready soon.

"I-I... How... Is that a song to get her to bang you?" I asked.

"Could be. I haven't decided if I wanted to change the pitch or not. It sounds slightly different with an octave higher or lower." he said.

"You... You wanna do it?" I blurted out. I don't fucking know why, it was just that smile, that comfortable attitude, that fuckin' awesome sound, that commanded nature to rise, and even made me rise a little. I started swearing at myself, then tried to tell him it was a fucking joke, but he said...

"I wouldn't want to hurt Yule like that. Thank you for the offer, Jake. That's very noble of you for being able to ask that question."

"...Noble?" I said.

"Well, it wasn't like Prince Charming or anything, but it takes guts to ask anyone that question, especially a close friend like we are." Lucius said.

"...You think I'm a close friend? Are you fucking making fun of me?" I said.

"No, Jake. I think of you as my friend. I don't know about a lover... but maybe-" he said.

My throat was constricting, I was feeling hot in my face, I said, "Ok, how do you want to do this? You bend over or me? Or sixty nine? How the fuck do homos work this angle?"

He just smiled, and said, "Maybe another day, Jake. I have to finish this song for my woman bound to me for life."

He continued playing, and all the animals came back, with me just as enthralled as them. I swear all of them wanted to hump him just as much as I did-

Cass yelled, "Sooey, Jake! Come an' get it, Lucius!"

"Food! Hell yeah, Cass and Lux are somehow great at making the dishes out of ramen packets and fat squirrels!" Lucius said, got up, scattering the squirrels on his lap, pet the doe on the head, and walked off to the food.

I just stared at his butt, flabbergasted.

Did I really just say all the shit I did?

I tried to eat the food, scared as fuck Lucius would tell anyone, but he didn't. It was like nothing had changed.

I thought... damn. So that's what it means to be romanced. It sure wasn't seduction, it was just... romance.

I slept with Cass in our tent, she hugged me tight, and we just slept, as I remembered that haunting music that even romanced me.

65

Dina

Some people can tell what true pain is. Some don't need to be told every little detail to see the full picture. Some are so attuned with the world, that they can feel its very bones shake at the slightest tremor, or if you're having a bad day even if you try to hide it with everything you've got.

I knew the world was in pain, I knew it was in suffering, as a monster tried to force his way on the very Earth.

Well, that monster was about to be homeless.

I roared with my might, conquering through Hell with legions of the damned. I made treacherous pacts and unholy alliances, and I raised my giant demonic axe over my head that I had won from beating a demon just by myself. And the demons respected me for it.

I really don't know what will happen when I kill the Devil… but he sure won't be coming back here.

After the battle, I wiped the demon blood off my face, and passed by my generals with my advisor.

There was Beleth, who could raise the demons into a frenzy with one demonic note, or one word that was soon echoed into a chant and shrieked by legion.

There was Darcy, a real bitch of a succubus, but one who finally gave up on going back to Earth, and preferred her eternal torment in Hell.

There was Georgia, another succubus, who was more of a spy than a warrior. I still hated her for causing Paul so much suffering in his life, as she molested him as he was a young boy.

There was Molech, a minotaur, who never said a single word, as Yule had taken his very tongue. He charged on the front, a once god of pagans.

And then there was my advisor, Sax, who had been the King of Hell before he made penance.

"Excellent job in weakening their flank, Darcy." I said.

"I always was a master at picking away at my prey... They never see it coming..." Darcy said.

"I will though, so drop that sinister note, and organize my troops into formation. These demons are undisciplined, and I expected better out of you."

"As you command, Oh Queen of Hell..." Darcy said, and bowed, then sauntered away to bring order.

"What can you tell me about the ones loyal to Satan, Georgia? We are vastly outnumbered." I said.

"They are foolishly bickering amongst themselves, as they always do. I gave them a few lines to keep them that way for another few lifetimes. They are terrified of your rule, fearing an even worse existence than under Satan." Georgia said.

"Excellent. There's always a different place to go to, even than the lowest Hell." I said.

"To be in a worse place than Hell... It sounds like poetry, Miss Dina." Beleth said.

"I didn't say worse. Just different." I said.

"I love a change in tune. Allow me to play for you in your quarters alone when we get a chance, to celebrate our impending victory." Beleth said.

I smiled, and said, "No thanks, Beleth. I don't plan on mating with a demon the same way Paul's mother was forced to."

"If you insist..." Beleth said, and bowed.

I simply nodded at Molech, and he nodded back.

"Come, Sax. Let us adjourn to discuss our next assault." I said, and the gentle looking man beside me followed me into my tent of war.

"I... really don't like being here all that much..." Sax said across from me at the table.

"You don't have to stay, if you don't want to. But your assistance is most welcome. I don't think I would've found my way through Hell half as easily without you." I said.

"I understand. And I really do want to help. So I will. It is just another step in my long road of penance..." he said.

"I thought you were forgiven and had made the proper amends?" I said.

"No, Miss Dina... for if you truly want forgiveness... Penance never ends." Sax said.

"Sin is an eternal stain. It's surprising people commit so many of them." I said.

We talked about our troops, the location we were situated in currently, and even had a spirited conversation on the origin of Hell and its many forms in different religions and cultures. I was going to be ruler of every one of them.

I dismissed Sax, and relaxed for a second, smoking another of Zax's cigarettes, and rubbed my belly, anxious for the child that would one day be my pride and joy.

But it was time to get back to work.

We approached the innermost of Hell, conquering the truly evil. A few demons held onto their scraps of brimstone and dirt, their damned territories, with all their might, before we forced them to submit to my will. A few of the truly suffering, the lost and confused who roamed Hell for eternity... were shown mercy by Sax and I. We allowed those few to go to Purgatory, to make amends for their mistakes.

Sax called upon a few of his friends and other caretakers of Purgatory, and angels guided these few out of Hell. This young woman and her husband were the most peaceful angels of them all. She, Angelica Nestor, always gave me a big bag of biscottis whenever I met her again, kind of like... a kindly old grandmother.

I gasped when I saw one of the angels with his back turned to me, as he helped an old, wicked sinner to Purgatory. By his black hair, by everything about him... he looked like Zax.

"Paul!" I shouted, running over to him, "Thank you for aiding us in these times of crisis."

He looked at me, and he looked grim. He said, "This is a difficult choice for me, Dina. I don't know what you will do with Hell when it is yours, but if I can help other damned people as I once was, then I will."

"Thank you. That is my goal as well." I said.

"The allies you've surrounded yourself with are true evil. They've killed and tortured many, in just Yule and my life alone." Paul said.

"We will all get our just reward at the end, and I see something valuable in these villains." I said.

"Don't lose yourself in Hell, Dina." Paul said, and he carried the weary sinner to Purgatory, flapping away on his majestic white wings.

And I turned back to my allies, and told them it was time to march.

I rode a demonic dragon, the one that St. George had defeated himself, actually also put down by Max as well, and the dragon and I roared through the sky of Hell, with my legions of demon soldiers marching in ordered unity under me through the underworld.

Beleth sang, and the demons roared for me, chanting together,
"Hellish grasp and evil's clasp,
Hoorara Hoorara!
Breaking bones and burning homes,
Hoorara Hoorara!
The Devil will lose his hated soul,
The Queen of Hell will come for you
The Queen of Hell will conquer you
The Queen of Hell will eat your soul.
Hoorara Hoorara!"

66

Yule

I asked Lucius, "Are you really Lucifer?"

"...That's an odd question, Yule." Lucius said.

"But you know things you shouldn't know. You're just as devilish as the most evil demon. You're somehow smart, nice, friendly, and extremely lovable. I don't really believe it." I said.

"Would it be better if I... *talked like this?*" he said.

My heart beat faster, as he looked at me calmly.

"Sorry, Yule. I'm not the pain of your past. We've only ever been in love, and tried to move past our own pains. You've felt the Devil's dark fire, and I can only say that you never have to feel it again with me." he said.

"...How can I be sure?" I said.

He shrugged, and said, "Have faith. I'll change my name for you, if you want. I don't need to be Lucius. Man... I never thought of that. Lucius the Lucifer."

"No. You don't have to change anything. I just... It's hard to give up the pain of the past." I said, and held his hand.

"It's really a very easy trick talking like a demon. They're just cold, heartless, and are easy to replicate when you've felt that cold heartlessness before." Lucius said.

"...Can you do it again?" I said.

"*You will be eternally tormented, in extreme pain, when I fuck you with lots of my dick.* It also helps to be crude and swear a lot when talking like a demon." Lucius said.

I giggled, and said, "I'm glad you can make me feel better like this."

"I lost my virginity to a demon girl." Lucius said.

"...What?" I said.

"She was just someone else in the foster home. I don't even understand how demons can be young adults, but she was. You know demons were considered normal people for a long time, before they showed their true colors." Lucius said.

"...I'm sorry." I said.

"It was painful, and awful, but I thought it was normal. She-" Lucius said.

"You don't have to talk about it. Or bring it up, or anything." I said.

"She tortured me in awful pain. In humiliation, in agony. But I thought that was love." Lucius said.

I held his hand sadly, as he frowned slowly, and I said, "I will treat you better. I will show you love as an angel should. You never have to feel that again with me."

He smiled gently, and said, "Thank you. I don't ever want to feel like a demon. I want to someday be like you, and be an angel."

"The first love is never the last, and I want to love you now. Talk like a demon, let it out." I said, and took him to the tent.

"But... I know that hurts you, and that hurts me." he said.

"No. I want to get over it. Talk like the most profane demon of Hell, and we'll fuck until we feel like we're in Heaven." I said, and took off his shirt in our tent.

"*...Sweetie?*" he said.

I smiled, and said, "You are just the sweetest. *Lucifer.*"

We laughed, rolled around with each other, and conquered our hellish fears, because I knew that no one else could make me feel this way, besides Lucius.

We climaxed as I called him sweetie, and he called me the Devil in disguise.

"You're the Devil in disguise... you got red eyes...

You must be somethin' good, but I don't know why...

You take me to Heaven, as I take you to Hell...

I love you sweetie, and we'll be the most of all...

You're my woman bound for life, and we'll fuck them all..." Lucius sang.

"I love you, Lucius. And we'll always be together. We can say fuck them all, and be happy in life, instead of Heaven or Hell." I said.

"That's good enough for me. We don't have to marry, or anything, just spend some life together for a while." Lucius said, and smiled. Nothing demonic about his smile, or his offer. Satan actually asked me to marry him, but Lucius... he was my man bound to me for life.

Fuck yeah! Sweetie was Lucius's name for me now, and not some asshole little prick Devil's!

And I was his Devil in disguise, me, an angel on Earth.

We loved again, and used our real names, our lovely, human names. Yule and Lucius, bound to each other for life.

I whispered in his ear how I got the name Yule... that really, it had always been my name. That my mother called me that in the Yule season, and it stuck over Hund, or anything related to dogs. My last name was Botschaft, Message in German, but translated to Tidings by me. The same way I converted to Christianity from my pagan tribal beliefs, I converted my name into Tidings to fit in with the modern day.

"I love you, Yule." he said, and we smiled, and hugged, and kissed.

We heard Jake singing with Elvis, in his voice that cracked when he tried to hit the notes, singing, "You're the Devil in disguise..."

67

Zax

"You should really just stop trying to sing that, Jake." I said to him.

"...Wha'? But I can do it, I know it. Why?" Jake said, resting his guitar in his grip.

"Well, it kinda hurts my ears, and it sounds like it's hurting your throat." I said.

"...I knew I shoulda never let Yule strangle me... Now I've got a fucked up voice..." Jake said, looking down at his guitar.

"Maybe it's all the other stuff too... But you've still got great fingers. How about you use those instead?" I said.

Cass overheard us, and came over to us and said, "Yeah, my girl's got great fingers. She always makes *me* sing when she uses them... Play us something, Jane."

Jake smiled at her, even though I didn't really know if she was making a joke at his expense. Jake just played... and then sang something in a womanly voice, like a goddamn chick's.

I was surprised as I heard him sing soprano, singing something close to that of Ave Maria but not quite.

I just sat with Cass, and listened to Jake sing, making up every verse and singing swears in between as he played guitar.

"I'llll fuck you in the buttttt girrrrrlll...

Ifff that's what you waaaaaannttt...

I'llll love you all dayyyyy and nigggghttt..

And we'lllll fuck jus' riiiiightttt...

Flippp me over baby, and use your robotlllyyy hannndsss....

And fuck me as you liiiike, baby, all niggggghttt...

Aveeeee Marrrrrrrrria......."

We clapped when he was finished, and he bowed.

"Ok. I take it back. Despite the crude lyrics, you've got a great voice, Jake." I said.

"Thanks. I won't ever be able to sing like you, but I can try. Maybe in a higher pitch... but whatever." Jake said.

"It took a long time to get to that point. I have faith in you. I smoke constantly, but I still played brass instruments as a child growing up, so increased my natural lung capacity as well." I said.

"So you're a tromboner?" Jake said, and grinned.

"I suppose. The more accepted term is trombonist, but I hear both. I've also been a trumpeter, a hornist..." I said.

Jake giggled, and Cass started laughing.

"...What? Those are the correct terms." I said.

Cass hit me on the arm forcefully, and said, "You horny hornist. It's nice seeing you out of the tent like this, instead of masturbating all day thinking of Dina."

"...How did you know?" I said.

The two just laughed some more, and Cass wrapped on arm around my shoulder, kissed my cheek, and said, "She'll be back for you. Come with me to the tent, I want to show you something."

I followed Jake and Cass to their tent, nervous. I didn't know how I would have a threeway with these two-

But Cass just came back out and handed me a full picture of Dina, as she was, a new picture of her with a flat chest... completely nude and posing erotically. Cass said, "Lucius took this of her because she asked him to. She really wanted to surprise you with it, but was unable to."

I stared at the picture, and I felt my heart skip. She was eternally winking in the picture, just for me.

Jake said, "Lucky Lucius. I never thought o' that... Be a fuckin' photographer, jus' so you can see the chicks posing for you... Fucking smart ass devil..."

Cass then handed me a bottle of lube, and said, "...And this might help too."

I smiled, hugged her, and said, "Thank you."

I then went to my tent, clutching my gifts.

It felt like she was really with me.

I fell asleep in comfortness, naked after I was done...

And I could've sworn I heard her say... that she was.

I woke up awake, and looked around the tent.

I was alone.

I prayed to see her again, nude as I was... I asked God to take me to Hell to be with Dina.

And somehow...

I knew that I would achieve this dream.

68

Lux

"You brought Yule back to life. Is there any way you can send me to Hell?" Zax asked me.

"...You want me to kill you or something? Can't you just commit suicide? That would be the easier route, and would probably land you in Hell." I said.

"...Uh... No. I don't want to die. I just want to be with Dina." Zax said.

"This is a very difficult conundrum, Zax... I *did* know how to bring demons to life from Hell-" I said.

"Can you bring Dina back?" Zax said.

"No. She wasn't a demon, and I do not believe she is. I... actually deleted all of my knowledge of hellish, heavenly, or dead person electricity. Can't you use your knowledge?" I asked.

"Everything I studied from SSS's, your creator's, knowledge I left in Friendliness. I brought the Devil to life to imprison him, and in the end it was the worst mistake of my life, and ended many people's lives. I do not want to make the same mistake. But you brought Yule back to life. You must've done something I couldn't." Zax said.

We looked over at Yule, who was playing Jake's guitar with Lucius playing flute. Cass and Jake sat watching them, cheering for them, Jake's arm over Cass's shoulder and her's around his waist.

I said to Zax, "When you look at Yule, what do you see?"

"...I see a happy, normal human." Zax said.

"And she was a dead human at one point. The body she has now is completely synthetic, crafted by me. Her soul originated as an angel of Heaven's that landed back on Earth, then she died and I trapped her soul into this body by luring her with a familiar form. There is no way to make actual life without taking from another's, besides the age old and tested by evolution practice of reproduction." I said.

"...But you seem like you're alive. If you had flesh, I'd say you were as human as me." Zax said.

"I find that kind of insulting, but also slightly endearing. The point I'm trying to make is that I did not create Yule naturally. I stole her soul from the abyss. This caused many unrectifiable consequences as well, starting with Yule herself." I said.

"But you gave her a chance at life again. Should she not be happy for that?" Zax said.

Yule came over, put an arm around my shoulder, and said, "Whatcha talking about, guys?" as the rest of our band played with Cass rapping.

I said, "Zax would like to bring Dina out of Hell, or go to Hell himself."

Zax said, "Not in a dead way!"

Yule said, "I thought I told you to try and continue your life. You'll see her again if you just let things happen... naturally."

Zax said, "I don't even understand how anything I did, anything Dina does, is natural. I am living this life with you all to try and return to my roots... But it seems impossible. I always have this unnatural handcuff on my wrist..."

"Ah yes." I said, "The demonic spark in that machine will never go out... Eternally charged and locked tight with its own electricity... Do you want me to try to take it off?"

"I've tried for a long time, using any possible solution. If I destroy it, it would explode and engulf me in flames. What do you think you could do?" Zax said.

"Water won't work, smashing it won't work, and it will continue to burn living material for as long as the matter has fuel. I *do* know how to nullify demonic electricity however, which I figured out how to do by giving Yule her wings. Simple, really. You just calculate pi by the square root of infinity divided by..." I said, and continued down the line, as Zax understood as best he could, nodding after every bit of mathematics. Yule walked away, bored of our mathematic prattle.

"...It's that easy? It almost broaches onto a religious ritual in a way. But what if you..." Zax said, and continued down his own theoretical route, with me suggesting ideas here and there.

And then... my. I never thought of it like that. It clicked for both of us, like a spark of electricity, and we gasped. I said, "That is incredibly dangerous, Zax. And could be the whole scheme of the Devil's."

"I don't care. Who knows why the Devil does anything, anyway? He's just an asshole who wants our souls so he can break them some more. If we believe everything put against us is someone else's twisted scheme, we'll never get anything done. But I need to try this." Zax said.

"Maybe you should... take a cat's perspectives, as you know... curiosity killed the cat. A scientist's greatest enemy is the knowledge that he strives for, because once you bring it into the world... it can never be unbrought. Unless you're like me, and delete it with a flip of a switch." I said.

"I will think it over for a while. But if I can unlock the gates of Hell with this key to free Dina, then I will." Zax said, and walked away, scratching the cat's back as the cat followed him with the dog.

69

Doug

Rasputin was so nice to me, even being a snarky cat. He knew it would be my time soon… Damn cats, I don't know how they don't keel over as soon as they eat a bad rat. But I could feel it in my bones, in the wind… I've lived a long time, for a dog, and I've had a rough life.

I spent the longest time living under savage humans who expected me to be as savage as them. So I became even worse. I killed anything put against me, any animal or human in that pit. I fought, but I survived. Until Dina saved me from that fate.

I was about to maul her, as she stared into my eyes. And no, they weren't black eyes. They were gentle, normal human eyes. I distinctly knew she was different than the other people, I could just see it in her soul, and I knew she lived in a cage just as I was in the cage she released me from.

We ran into the night, her from her ex, my old "master," and me protecting my new savior in any possible way. I nearly slaughtered her ex when he tried to reclaim me, but that man, who went by the name of Vindicta, was the one who turned me into what I was, and beat me away.

I would've kept gnashing at him, no matter how hard he hit me, as I was trained by him to do so, but Dina called me a name. She called me Doug, when I was just a dog, and so I followed her, leaving Vindicta bleeding out on the pavement. Sadly, he survived, but he became an influential figure for the people of Friendliness after the world went to hell, so I suppose it was a good thing I inadvertently showed mercy.

It was just us two, Dina and Doug, for a long time. I didn't even let anyone into her apartment, and she actually became accustomed to such an overbearing protection. No one was allowed near me or her, when I was with my friend, Dina.

Until she brought in an angel through her door. I snarled at Yule like every other, but the angel called me a good boy, and I could tell she wasn't nearly accustomed to showing suffering as others.

Although she lived in a pit as much as I did, in her old life. As much as Cass did as well, in her current life. Us three were friends, and we all lived in cages before.

Now... as soon as I finally feel the cage leave my body... I will leave my body as well.

Rasputin revealed his smart cat nature to Zax in the woods, and convinced Zax to think it over *hard.* That perhaps unlocking this cage will let a lot of horrible things out.

I did feel kind of bad for the demons, and I did miss Dina, but perhaps... the cage is best. I knew if anyone could make the demons feel like they weren't in a cage anymore, it would be Dina. Perhaps she would be able to show them that the true cage of life isn't physical, but a mental cage.

I went to be alone, hiding in an alcove of tree roots, to pass.

I shut my eyes... and someone pet my fur.

I opened them, and an angel of death smiled to me, and I barked playfully to him. I got into his pale car, and stuck my head out the window as we began driving.

"You're a good boy, Doug." Max said to me, and I howled in happiness as we ascended to Heaven.

70

Cass

"Doug! C'mon, boy! Come and play!" I yelled out. The cat kept rubbing against me, and seemed like he wanted me to follow him, so I did.

I cried as Rasputin showed me Doug's dead body.

I left him there, and came back with a spade.

I dug a pit for Doug, crying the whole time, and buried his body in the earth.

I wiped off my tears, scratched the cat's back, and shambled back to camp.

I just cried and cried, looking on at that sunset. Jake held my hand, and simply sat with me. "He was a good boy. Even though I could do absolutely nothing to him when he came into the tent, couldn't kick 'im out, couldn't do shit. He'd just stare at me with tha' one eye, and I knew my life would end if I touched him." Jake said.

"He was just like me, in a way… Touch us wrong, and we'd kill you…" I said, sniffling.

"…Yeah. You both have wild spirits in you, and I'm sure Doug's spirit is being wild still." Jake said.

I squeezed his hand even tighter, and I think something crunched. His face went white, but he didn't try to escape my grip.

He started to say, "Motherfuckingjesuschristamen-"

But I stopped him by crying and looking into his eyes.

He said, "...Sorry. I thought that would make you feel better."

"No... I don't want to feel happy now. I want to be sad, and let my sadness be. Thank you, though. It's always the I love you part which gets me, anyway." I said.

"...Really? So the whole fucking magic word... is just I love you?" he said.

"Kinda. It just makes me feel happy, hearing you say that." I said.

"I love you then, Cass." he said.

I smiled sadly at him, kissed him on the cheek, and said, "I love you too, Jake."

"You mean Jane?" he said.

"No. I'm getting sick of the whole girlfriend fantasy, anyway. Girls are bitches, and frankly you aren't a bitch at all. Sure, sometimes you're a rude fucking dick, but not a bitch." I said.

"Ok. I guess that's a compliment? I don't know if it's better to be a dick or a bitch." Jake said.

I shrugged, and said, "Try to not be either, ok?"

"...Sure. Do you need anythin' to relax? I've learned a few things from you, and I can just give you a massage if you like." Jake said.

"That sounds nice. My workout session leaves my back kind of sore, anyway." I said.

We held hands back to the tent, where he massaged my back.

I felt happy as he said my magic words, caressing my back. I love you.

We fell asleep together, and I dreamed... I was pretty good at being lucid... but this one, I didn't really know if it was real or not, it was so terrible.

I stood on a ledge in the darkest, most horrible fiery pit of Hell. I saw legions of demons roaring and shouting, chanting something awful and evil. I saw the succubi lead their unholy army, I saw a godish monster charge with his shock troops, and the singer... I was terrified of such an evil sounding music. There was some gentle looking man trailing from behind, and he looked up, and I followed his gaze.

I saw Dina riding a dragon, and each of them roared, one in fire, the other an angry woman's scream.

I followed at a distance, watching this unholy spectacle, walking through horrible looking trees that whispered evil to me, dead trees that always seemed to get in my way. I just followed Dina's trail of fire in the sky and in Hell.

I peeked through some dead trees, and saw a single demon sitting cross legged in the center of a circle. Dina's troops circled this circle, and Dina dropped from the dragon to face this demon.

The Devil stood up, flapped his golden, shredded wings, and said in his satanic voice, *"Welcome to Hell, Dina. You've just lived out your worst hell, killing and conquering for nothing. You've come to take Hell from me, but you only brought more endless suffering. I congratulate you on such evil."*

Dina said, "Enough, Lucifer. You will be brought down eternally by me. We will end this now."

Satan cackled, and said, *"Evil will always live. Even if you take my evil away... You will take my place."*

"I believe not. Hell is just another life, and can be brought to goodness as well. Molech, bind this monster." Dina said.

"Yes, Molech... bind this monster." Satan said.

The big cow head godish creature smashed Dina on the back of head, suckerpunching her.

I screamed, and Dina looked at me before she lost consciousness.

I kept screaming, even as Jake told me it was just a dream and I was awake.

71

Jake

I looked over at Yule watching the sea, saying goodbye to it before we left. Lucius, Lux, Zax and I were packing up, as Cass... shook in the van, frightened of somethin'. It made me scared too, because she wasn't afraid o' nothing.

Yule waved at the sea one last time, an' walked over to us, sayin', "Well. Let's do something productive with our time, guys. Let's start a band."

I said, "Fuckin' really?? I've been horning in that question whenever I could, but you all seemed to ignore me."

Zax said, "I suppose that will be a better use of my time than going to Hell..."

Lucius said, "I think that's a great idea. It's a peaceful way of showing happiness to people, helping to save them in a way, one song at a time."

Lux said, "I like it too. Did you all see my drum set?? It's really coming along nice!"

I said, "...It's very interestin', Lux. I think it only works cuz your hands are so metally and give off the perfect sound, too."

Lux said, "I think it's nice. There's always so much more sounds to make, and I'd really like to experiment with them all. By hitting them! I never knew my force could be used like this, instead of using it to crush skulls."

Yule said, "Yeah, well, let's see if we can find some people to play for. Lucius, take the wheel."

I said, "...But he'll kill us."

"Nah." Yule said, "He's maybe just a little rusty, but he knows how to drive."

I grumbled, as Lucius grinned.

I told him to slow down as he sped down the road, blasting some sort of hip hop beat from the radio that was accompanied by a flute.

He ignored me, swerving at each turn. Yule laughed from the passenger seat, as I sat next to Cass as she trembled.

I thought I'd die. I never thought I could nearly be dead jus' by lettin' this wild man drive.

I eventually *sort of* got used to it, and kept telling Lucius what to do, but he said, "Quit being a backseat bitch, Jake! Enjoy the speed!"

I shut up. I just clutched Cass, as I trembled as well.

Lux and Zax were talking about some mathy crap, but I think it had something to do with music because they always talked about "resonance."

We drove down the plains road, and my heart stopped as Lucius began driving down the plains.

I couldn't even make a sound, I was so scared. Fucker was driving offroad down the plains.

And then Cass noticed somethin' out the window, and said, "Hey guys. What is that?"

I peeked out where she was peeking, and saw a thing. Something. I don't know. But it had a long mane... four strong legs and a long neck...

Yule said, "That's a horse, guys."

Cass said, "No fucking way!! I thought they went extinct?? Oh my God... Should we eat it?"

I looked at that wild horse, so beautifully free. It ran back to a few others, in a pack or a band or whatever you call a group of horses, herd, yeah, and I said, "No. Let's... Let's jus' look at 'em."

Lucius stopped the van, and we looked at the horses.

Cass said, "I want to catch one of those, one day. They're so pretty!"

I said, "I... I want to drive one of them. Or something? Can you... They look so fast! I'd love to have that speed on my legs."

Yule said, "Sure, guys. I'll show you how to ride a horse."

Yule gently approached the horse, as it stared at her. It looked like it was about to run off... but that crazy albino did something miraculous. She ran up to it, and jumped onto the horse's back,

The horse kicked and neighed, but Yule hung onto it for a good long time, before it eventually bucked her off.

Lucius ran over to her, helped her up, as she laughed and dusted herself off. The horses ran off into the distance.

Wow.

I've only ever heard of the things, mares buckin' and kicking, but wow. They really do put up a fight. I thought a mare was just an expression for a woman.

And I would make that wild mare, that gorgeous untamed horse, mine. Cass held my hand, and she said, "What if we had that farm you mentioned? But not only with pigs. What if... we had horses?"

I squeezed her robot hand, even though she couldn't feel it, and said, "I love you, Cass."

"You'reasexysonofabitchwithabigfuckingdickIloveyouJakelet'sfuck." she whispered in my ear.

And wow. I just came in my pants.

Lucius said as they got back to us, "Holy shit! That was awesome! That was even cooler than me driving for the first time like I just did!"

"It was so much fun! I've only ever ridden a horse with someone else before, but never jumped on a wild one by myself!" Yule said.

I said, "...Wha'? You both did that for the first time?"

Lucius and Yule laughed, and Zax said, "Hey guys... there's a building over there. It looks... populated. Maybe we can play for them?"

Lux said, "It seems to be an old school. Let's all be very careful, just in case, and we can scout it out."

We hid the van behind a hill, and began conversin' on scouting tactics.

72

Yule

"I'll go in. If anyone tries to mess with me, I'll slice them in half." I said.

Lucius said, "I could just sneak in a bit? Let me scout it out."

I said, "But what if you don't come back, if you go in alone? We'll never know what happened to you. I don't want to risk you like that."

Lucius said, "I can see how that makes sense."

Lux said, "I could go. If you all haven't noticed, I am basically impervious."

Zax said, "But what if you're not? They could've figured out some way to kill you, and may open fire on you as soon as they see a robot approach them. Don't trust in your own infallibility."

Lux said, "I guess. I'm glad you all care about my life so, as I do to you all."

Zax said, "I could just light the thing on fire, smoke 'em out, and see what awaits us…"

Cass said, "That sounds very mean, Zax. They're probably nice people, and we should just give them a gift or something first."

Jake said, "We're basically fuckin' defenseless if they try to take our gift and kill us anyway. I seriously don't know how we've survived for so long with only a hatchet, a machete, and Yule's samurai sword. Guess we got lucky."

Cass said, "I think if we just leave a present on their doorstep? One gift at a time?"

Jake said, "Let's all go in together, guys. We all got each other's backs. Let's be safer as a group."

Rasputin mewled.

The rabbit, Clippers, turned on the TV, and said, "Can I aid you?"

Jake said, "Yeah. A ghost could help scout out the surroundin'. I really don't see how you fucking work, rabbit."

Clippers said, "It will be my pleasure to aid you as you traverse the-Something."

Clippers hopped out of the TV, and I pet him as he hopped into my arms. I said to him, "Be careful, Clippers."

Clippers said, "I'll let you see through my eyes, Yule. You'll be able to see what I see."

I hopped- Clippers hopped out of the van, and I saw him sneak up on the building.

He snuck in through a window, and looked around the halls of the school.

We heard whimpering, and I urged Clippers to check it out.

We hopped to the basement, a hidden basement in the back of a classroom...

We looked down the dark steps, and heard the sound of children crying.

Then a demon ascended from the dark basement, looked at Clippers, and said, "...Ghosts?"

Clippers ran as fast as he could out of the building, got in the van, and hopped back into the TV, and shut himself off.

I felt furious anger. There were children in that place, trapped by demons. I told my band we would do anything we could to save them, and they all agreed.

We looked out the van, because someone was approaching us. A woman with a machine gun. She looked terribly fierce, had red hair, and called out to us, "C'mon out, kids. It's time to go to school."

The six demons followed behind her, and we were soon surrounded as they snickered.

We got out of the van, and the woman aimed the gun at me as I tried reaching for my sword. I let my hands rest gently at my side, as she marched us into the building with her demons.

She locked us in a classroom, away from where I saw the children. I asked her who she was, and she said, "I am your teacher. And I will teach you how to be my slaves. Learn well, and I won't eat you instead. We're all hungry, and we can't lose another kid... The kids don't have enough meat on them, anyway."

I slammed my hands on the door, screaming in anger, and the red haired woman laughed.

Lucius asked, "...How did she get red hair?"

I said, "I don't know. But I'm going to kill her."

73

Teacher

I loved fucking with these stupid scavengers. It took me all my life to accumulate a group of demons to be my slaves. To teach them to obey. These stupid scavengers... Why would I eat a child? The stupid kids were just as bad as them. If they didn't have me they'd be dead. They'd be slaughtered by my demons.

I went down to them as they cried in the basement. "T-Teacher. When can we leave?" one of the children asked.

"You will leave when you have learned your lesson." I said.

They cried some more, as I threw the meat on the floor for them to grab at, eating carefully.

That was the last bit of our meat, so I suppose I'd have to kill that one tasty looking albino... Too bad. She looked so pretty and rare.

Or maybe the quiet man? The one who clutched his flute... I wanted that flute.

Or maybe the scarred guy. He frankly looked like he had something wrong with his meat, because he even had three eyes...

Maybe the black haired one... but I feel like if I tried to cook him, I'd get burned. He hasn't made a move yet...

Or I guess the cyborg. She did look the healthiest, although frankly no arms or legs of meat.

What the fuck could I do with a robot? I guess it would be fun to smash it.

The child said, "I will never leave... You want me to be your slave."

I said, "Congratulations. You've learned the lesson."

They burst out crying, as I smiled to myself and ascended the stairs.

Humanity was disabled, destroyed, nothing but scavengers, looters, cannibals... and me. I would use these shreds of humanity, with the monsters and evil tools we have acquired, so that we would survive. I would bring this world out of its hellish earth, and into a golden age again.

There were always people like me in history. But we usually change the textbooks to give us a more favorable account. There were always people who knew that it takes just a little extra measures to make the world people need.

I went to my quarters in the principal's office, and drenched my hair in blood. I hated my black hair, and this blood made a better color.

I told my six demons to be ready to kill the albino. I stroked the biggest, evilest demon's chin. I could not kill him myself like the others, so I commanded him with sex instead. He was my most loyal slave.

I aimed my machine gun at the door. These dumb scavengers didn't even have guns... Don't they know the world they live in? It's too bad they won't live it too much longer...

One by one, piece by piece, they will serve, or I will eat them, one by one, piece by piece...

A cat mewled at me from the side. A cat?

"Hello." the cat said.

"...Are you some sort of... What are you?" I asked it, as my demons and I stared at the cat.

"I am just a cat." the cat said.

"...Then how can you talk?" I asked.

"Well, I'm a cat." the cat said.

Getting frustrated with this creature, I shot the cat dead. I decided I'd like to eat some sort of magical animal too-

But the cat laughed and ran off.

Ok. That wasn't what cats usually did.

Did they?

74

Rasputin

I let the children pet me in this horrible basement. They were so happy to pet my fur, and I let them cuddle me.

I told them, "Be ready, children. Your teacher is coming, and we should teach her a lesson."

"B-But it's impossible to beat Teacher." one of the children said.

"Nothing is impossible. That's a very simple lesson to learn. My friends would fight and kill for you all, even burn this building down, but that would lead to your injury or theirs. I will distract Teacher, and then you will take her gun." I said.

"B-But… She's so scary." another child said.

"I know. But you need to be brave. I believe my friends can take care of the demons, but we just need to get her gun." I said.

The teacher stomped down the stairs into the basement, wielding her machine gun. She said, "Here, kitty, kitty, kitty…" as I blended into the shadows with my black and grey fur.

The children were frightened, but I helped give them courage.

I slashed at the teacher with my claws, she shrieked in pain and shot around me to try and kill me again.

I roared a cat's roar, and the kids attacked.

They were starved, emaciated, weak, but I kept on slicing at the teacher and made her bleed, and the kids took the gun from her hand.

They shakily aimed it at the teacher, and she said, "Enough, children. Give that back to your master."

"No. I am not a slave." the child with the gun said, and he shot his teacher dead. He would learn from better teachers, one day, and even learn from the life that had been deprived of him.

I led the kids out of the basement, and they blinked at the light. We then heard the roaring battle cry of Yule, after Cass had ripped the door down with her strength.

We saw one demon slashing and clawing at Lux, but Lux just crushed his skull.

Jake and Lucius fought together, as a pair, one slaughtering a demon with a machete, the other slaughtering another with a hatchet.

Cass boxed a demon to death, and she killed it with an uppercut.

Yule and the big demon were circling each other, but Yule blazed her six wings of fire out, causing true terror in this most evilest of these demons, and she decapitated him with one swing.

Zax did not use his flame, because he did not wish to set the building on fire, and the last demon ran off down the hall, escaping us to scream down into the plains.

Yule went to the children first, and hugged them gently. Lucius played a soft sound to calm the frightened children. The others took the children by the hand and showed them out of their prison.

I sat with the kids by the van who just pet me as they cried, but soon Zax started a tune for the kids.

"You'll be back in the world, with cats and dogs,

With hogs and horses, people in cars,

Happily playing, singing, and laughing,

No more darkness, no more meat,

We'll all be together, and dance to the beat." Zax sang.

Lux started playing drums, Jake brought out his guitar and played, Lucius played his flute, and Cass said, as she started dancing,

"We're gonna have a good time, a fine time,

Singin' and rappin' like a good sign,

Dance with me, dudes! Let's party!"

Yule pet me, as I rubbed against her legs, and she picked me up and danced with me in her arms.

I mewled at her, and she traded me off to the other kids, who danced with me in their arms as well.

It was our first and last performance, just for some lost children.

75

Dina

I was back where I started. A cell in Hell... but with Georgia watching me this time, instead of leaving me to rot by myself.

"You were fated for this from the beginning, 'Queen of Hell.' Now you know what it means to be eternally damned." Georgia said.

"I can get that. But... You know, there's always a different place to be." I said.

"What bullshit. I don't want to go to Purgatory, and every word of sorrow and repentance of mine would be a lie." Georgia said.

"Yes. You are good at lying. So... What do you want to do?" I said.

"I could rape you, if you like." Georgia said.

"Nah, thanks though. I was wondering why you gave up all that power... Even Darcy still has more power than you, now. But you... You're stuck guarding me." I said.

"...Darcy is just a cruel, dominant succubus. I get what I want, with other ways, and don't have to use such tactics as her." Georgia said.

"But you could, couldn't you? You'd really spend an eternity talking to me and threatening to rape me? I hear Darcy has already become Satan's consort..." I said.

"...*So? That's a shitty job. He's Satan. I sure don't want to be his consort.*" Georgia said.

"But you were, weren't you." I said.

"*Yes. And he let me die to go back to Hell. He damned me even if he thought I was valuable.*" Georgia said.

"So why don't you make him your consort? Why don't you turn the tables? Just because I couldn't, doesn't mean you can't." I said.

"*...He's got a dominant succubus watching his back. I cannot defeat Satan.*" Georgia said.

"But Darcy might be able to. And where does that leave you? Stuck guarding my cell. I'd stab her in the back if I were you, cause her some suffering for leaving you while she's got such a cushy job." I said.

"*...You make fair points. I'll start with doing this one thing... Unlocking your cell. Welcome to the damned life, dude. Enjoy it, because it is Hell.*" Georgia said, unlocked my cell, and walked away, like she could care less what happened to me.

I walked through the doors, and Darcy crept up on me as I was walking through the valley of death, but I could practically smell her coming. I turned to her, and she grinned from atop the dead tree.

Darcy said, "*Smart. Using a stupid succubus to let you see more of Hell. But you should've stayed in your cell. This whole place is a prison. I've tried to leave it forever... but I'm accepting my evil fate for my evil actions.*"

"You could make the most of it, instead of taunting me in a tree." I said.

She cackled, and said, "*You are weak. Even in life you were just a weak little girl, a little stripper. I had an entire company under me, I conquered men with my will. But you... you had no life experience whatsoever. And you thought you could be Queen of Hell??*"

"And look where all your life experience has gotten you." I said.

She jumped down from the tall tree, landing in front of me, and said, *"Do not cross me, 'Queen of Hell...' For you will be in even a worse Hell under me."*

"Too bad it's not really yours. You've submitted to your overlord... Now *that's* weak. I'm just taking a stroll through Hell, no master, no God or Devil, just me." I said.

She tried to put a hand to my face, but I caught her hand. She did not try to force her hand on me with her indomitable succubus strength, and just said, *"You should probably leave. I'm telling you this for your own good. You don't want to live in Hell."*

She took her hand away from me, and I said, "I think you should worry more about your own life, than mine. There could be a succubus waiting around the corner for you... Watch out."

She looked around her nervously, and I continued down the path in the valley.

I was taking a walk through this dead forest, and I heard some evil music stalking me.

I turned to Beleth, who said, *"I do think it is a shame you lost so one sidedly... I could do nothing, I assure you, as your army crumbled into fighting amongst itself..."*

"Strange. You were always the one who kept the most order with your chants and songs." I said.

He took my arm in his arm, as we continued to walk through the dead forest, and he said, *"It is a shame... but I was just so uninspired by your defeat, I couldn't think of a single note. Perhaps next time, you'll be able to listen to one of your generals' tunes, and not make such foolhardy alliances..."*

"I suppose. You're saying I should only have trusted you? I don't trust you, though." I said.

"Just remember, Dina... if you ever doubt me... I only play the final song. I do not play the opening act or second fiddle for any other. I play, the curtain closes... and we are done. Remember that, Miss Dina." Beleth said.

"Alright. I'll save that song for another day, perhaps. You can sing me the same song as you try to stab me in the back like the others." I said.

"Of course... Have a beautiful rest of your eternity..." Beleth said, and I walked through the forest alone as he continued down another route.

Molech stood before me, an indomitable god, only defeated by an angel of war on Earth, before I got to my destination.

He roared a moo at me, but I said, "Oh, just shut up already." and I turned him to stone under my dark gaze.

Two succubi were trying to stab each other in the back in the forest, wrestling and screaming, and I said, "You both don't want to leave. So you can stay here. Forever." I then turned them to stone with my eyes of black, and they were eternally locked together.

I stepped in the middle of the forest, the middle of Hell, and claimed my victory. My greatest enemies were my closest allies, and I kept them closer than my friends.

I waved to Sax, who always did trudge at the back, afraid of his choice to help me, and he knelt before me, and claimed me Queen of Hell. He tried to offer his allegiance, but I said, "You never belonged to me, Sax. You belong to God."

Sax got up from kneeling, and we hugged each other. He flew back off to Purgatory with his tiny wings, to help other sinners make amends.

Satan had seen the whole thing, but he vanished before I turned my gaze on him as well.

76

Satan

They were all watching me. Every little person, God, all of them... They were watching me like her.

I fell for my pride, and they all saw me fall.

I didn't really care.

But now that one woman is watching me. And I feel like something else is too.

I watched as Yule and Lucius reclaimed the abandoned school. They cleaned the place up and made the once prison into a home.

I watched as Jake and Cass actually caught a horse, Jake riding the wild mare as Cass screamed in delight.

I watched as Lux began teaching the children what he knew, to help them live in a better world.

The cat saw me, as I watched Zax go into the forest alone, as I stalked Zax.

I ran from such an unholy creature as an unlucky cat, crossing my path in the shadows I lived in.

I chased after Zax. If I could not have Heaven, could not have Hell, I will at least claim this man's soul. He was my greatest challenge, since his forebear escaped from me once, A HALF DEMON. He should've been mine from birth, and his story is haunting me still, the story I was the archnemesis for.

I do not want to be a hero. The world will always need villains. You wouldn't try to live so hard if someone didn't try to take your life and soul.

I followed Zax, as he used his key on a portal of Hell for only him, a portal I had just walked out of, impervious, unknowable, unseeable to all.

But he used his key, my manacle on him, which had no value whatsoever. It was simply a strong manacle, with a few hellish fiery tricks of mine.

He said to the door, some sort of password, "I love you, Dina."

His manacle broke off his wrist, falling to the dirt, and the door crumbled open before him, and he passed down into Hell.

I was watching almost as much as God, before, unless you got too boring.

But now you are watching me.

I enjoy being the center show.

But not as a scared rat.

I ran down the road, but I would make my final stand. Let you all see the fall of Lucifer again.

For one day you may be just like me.

77

Zax

The world did not need villains. The world only needed other people, animals, plants, life, to love, to show love for and to show love to us.

I left that life behind, descending down into unlife, to be with the one woman I desired, the one woman I loved.

I said my goodbyes, but truthfully I think the others thought I was only going to walk in the forest, and come back one day.

If I tripped down these endless stairs, I would've died. What would happen to me if I died in Hell?

I talked to the boatman to take me over the river Styx. We actually had a nice conversation on cheese. *"Love me some good cheese."* Charon said. I never expected that, and instead of giving him a coin to take me over the river, I gave him a block of cheese in my pocket that we had looted ages ago. I didn't have any worthless currency on me, anyway. What was more valuable to us nowadays was food.

Charon snacked on my cheese as we crossed the river.

I was prepared for anything, prepared to run, prepared to fight…

But a few demons just waved to me, smiling cheerfully.

I walked over to this odd damned couple, who were building a house. "What are you doing?" I asked.

"The Queen of Hell is giving us permission to build! I never had an actual house before, even if it's made of brimstone!" the demon man said.

The demon woman said, *"Oh, dear. You know we could never afford one. We were merciless serial killers, not famous musicians."*

The demon man said, *"This will be a blast! I can't wait to lure someone into our trap house so we can kill them again and again and again!"*

The demon woman said, *"Oh, dear. You just have the sexiest mind. Care to help us, stranger? You can be the first one we kill!"*

I quickly walked away.

This is not what I expected of Hell. I expected torture and screaming in pain, not screaming in delight with demons killing each other playfully and building things everywhere.

I walked into a spooky forest, scared of the trees that seemed to be stalking me, but letting me pass.

I got to a woman standing in the center of a circle, smoking a- smoking one of my cigarettes, staring at a few odd statues.

I ran to her, crying, "Dina!"

A dragon landed from the sky in front of me, and snarled. A horrible, demonic looking dragon.

"It's ok, dragon. Zax!! Are you dead?? You don't look like you are in the least! I love you, Zax!" Dina screamed and ran over to me, where we hugged each other, and kissed.

"No, I'm alive. I just wanted to see you again." I said.

She looked at me quizzically, and said, "Really? You came down to Hell... For me? That sounds incredibly stupid for a short relationship like we had."

"Er... I don't think so. You saved my soul from-" I started.

"I saved your soul from falling to Hell, Zax. But look where you are! Goddamnit..." Dina said, and threw her cigarette butt at the cowman statue.

My face went red, and I said, "I feel like that really doesn't matter anymore. You gave me my soul to keep, and I want to give it to you."

"Really... Why don't you marry me or something then? If you're so damned loving..." Dina said.

I smiled, went down on one knee, and asked her, "Will you marry me, Dina?"

Her face went red, she looked extremely frustrated, but she said, "Yes. Goddamnit... I broke your chains, and now I'm going to put on yours as well..."

"Call it a key. We have the key to our love, all we need to do is dream for it, and then we'll have it." I said.

She blushed even redder, and began kissing me as I was on my knees. I smiled and kissed her back.

"I've been having a lot of time to read down here. There's tons of evil books damned for eternity... but I really like the ones I snagged from that book shop ages ago. What do you think we should name our child? I'm thinking Ferdinand if he's a boy, Hanatrix if she's a girl." Dina said.

I smiled, got up from kneeling, and said, "Whatever you like. I'm glad you're so enthused by our new engagement. You're even planning on naming our future children already!"

"Er, you remember when you were basically in a coma? Well... the part of you I needed wasn't. So, it won't be in the *far* future or anything..." Dina said.

I looked at her quizzically, and then it hit me. I fell into her arms, and said, "I'm so happy for us. I love you, Dina."

She slowly hugged me back, and said, "I love you too, Zax. You will be a great father for my Queendom."

"I just hope to be a great father." I said and held hands with her.

"No. You will be my King of Everything. We will take over the entire creation and beyond-" Dina said.

"As long as I'm with you." I said.

"...You mean you don't want to take over everything with me?" Dina said.

"I don't think it's that important. We've got a great life to live in this strange... place. Unless you'd care to go back to the living world?" I said.

She called out to someone, and a demon appeared before her instantly, scaring the crap out of me.

Dina said, "Beleth. Postpone the invasion."

The demon said, *"...But everything is set to start."*

Dina said, "...I know. I just... I need a chance to think, and talk with my fiancé."

I looked at the demon who bowed to her and disappeared again, and Dina took my hand and we walked down the path away from the statues.

78

Lucius

We found tons of guns in the building. It was odd that the demons weren't using them, and the only one who was was that red haired woman.

But we cleaned the place up, threw out the corpses and burned them, scraped up the demon ashes after they burned up themselves, and allowed them peace. The children were frightened of the place in the beginning, but we showed them dorms instead of the basement, and they got used to having a real bed of their own. This place looked like it would need a lot of stuff, if it was ever going to be a proper home...

I propositioned to Yule, "Do you think we can help these kids? Do what we did for them, instead of just for ourselves?"

"Yes. I actually really love that idea, Lucius. We can make this school into a full fledged home, eventually." Yule said.

Lux said, "These children are lost, everyone they could've gone back to are dead... They will need someone to care for them, to help them learn how to fend for themselves. I will take this opportunity on for myself."

I said, "That does make the most sense. You know the most out of all of us, and I'm sure you could teach these kids while we find them goods."

Jake said, riding over to us on his horse, "I fuckin' can ride a horse now."

"I see that, Jake. Do you want to help us make this place into a good home for these kids?" I said.

"Fuckin'... kids... Well, alright. I was thinkin' we could start a ranch over down the road in that old farm or somethin', me and Cass. We could... I don't know... feed them? Fuckers have been eating human flesh for a long time... They need some good bread." Jake said.

Cass said, "I would love to care for these kids, in any way. And have my ranch. We'll be just down the road for you guys, and I can help do whatever we need to make this building strong again."

I said, "Are you just going to teach them how to fight? That wouldn't be a bad thing."

"Nah." Cass said, "I'm going to teach them how to build. Lux has been teaching me all I need to know about machinery, just for my own arms and legs, with me tinkering with them here and there. And fuck, I'm stronger than all of you, maybe besides Lux. I can use this might to make homes for these kids."

A kid came up to me, yanked on my sleeve, and said, "Dark Piper... Can you play us some music before bed? We're having a hard time sleeping."

"Of course, Samantha. I'll be right there." I said.

Samantha hugged me, and I let her walk off back to the dorm, safe.

"Well." I said, "I guess it's our time to depart, guys. Need a lift, Jake? Cass?"

Jake lifted Cass up onto his horse, his guitar and pack on his back, and said, "Nah. We'll be right down the road. We'll be fine. If you need anythin' don't hesitate to ask."

I went over to them, and shook Jake and Cass's hands, and said, "Good luck. We'll always be around for you two."

I looked at Yule, and she was crying.

"I don't want to see us all break up!! We never even named the band!!" Yule cried out.

"Er, Jake and I could never think of what to call it, and Zax... We know he's gone, like he said..." I said.

Yule said, "No. I'm going to bring them all back! I don't want you all to leave me! You all have been my best friends in this hard life!!"

Lux hugged her as she cried, and Lux said, "And you've got a long time to live to make more friends. You and Lucius find stuff for us, and we'll all be right here."

Yule said, "I'm going to find Dina and Zax first, and we'll name the band-"

We heard Dina say beside us, "Tidings of Tulips."

We turned, and saw Zax and Dina smile to us.

79

Cass

I jumped off the horse immediately! I ran to Dina and Zax and squeezed them both to death! I actually had to stop squeezing pretty soon, because it looked like they were losing circulation in their body.

"Dina! I'm so happy you're alive! How did you just... poof?" I said.

"I'm the Queen of Hell now, and Zax is my fiancé." Dina said.

"No way! You popped the question, Zax?? That's- That's amazing! I'm so happy for you both!" I said.

Zax felt Dina's belly, and said, "And we've got another on the way, for our family."

I gasped, and said, "I'm just so happy!! Even more! Come, we need to celebrate!"

Yule said, "...Queen of Hell?"

"I need to speak to someone that you can take me to, Yule. I need to speak to God." Dina said.

I said, "Oh, that's easy. Just clutch your hands in prayer and say-"

Dina said, "No, I mean like face to face. Just me and Yule."

I looked to Yule, and she looked very pale. I looked to Jake, who was looking quizzically at the whole thing. Jake said, "How'd she just... Forget it. I think we should let these magic people do their thing, Cass. It's great seeing you two again, so come visit us sometimes."

I said, "...But..."

"C'mon, babe. Let's let the big dudes talk. It'll be late soon, and we've gotta fortify that farm while we can." Jake said.

I looked at Dina, and she nodded. I hugged her one last time, and got back on the horse with Jake.

We rode off into the distance, happy for the speed. But I still felt kind of sad, despite the excitement of my new life.

We spent a long time building fortifications, I prayed for thanks for our new home, and we even set up a little fire in the fireplace in the cabin.

We sat together, me on Jake's lap, his arms around me, in this old rocking chair.

I smiled to him, and he smiled to me.

We would make our own dreams possible, because we finally each had a good person to spend them with.

And well, we really made lightning when we broke in our new home beside the flickering fire... nude...

I don't really care if you watch. But try to keep it a secret!

His big muscles bulged as he grabbed me up in his arms, his beautiful pride completely erect for me...

I stroked him with my metallic hand, I felt him just right, and my hand didn't get stuck this time. He grinned, and I flipped him over.

He was my wild stallion, and I would ride him for as long as I pleased, which happened to be a good long time.

Of course, we both said our magic words over and over, and couldn't stop from making love until we were exhausted and completely drained.

We sat by the fire, nude with each other, and we felt like our new life had just begun.

80

Yule

We spent a long time talking *how* exactly and *why* exactly Dina wanted to talk to God.

"I just don't want to make the mistake of a lifetime, and start something that I can't finish." Dina said.

I looked at her as I was frustrated, but I said, "There's only one way besides dying that you'll be able to get to see God. We can go up. Hop into my arms, and I'll do what I never tried to do. We can fly to Heaven."

Dina shook a little bit, as I held her in my arms, and I rocketed my wings from my back, she waved to the others, and we launched into the sky.

She clung to me for a long time, but eventually relaxed as we burst through the clouds. She said to me, "You were my first real love, Yule."

"I know... And I'm proud of that. I'm glad I could be with you and Cass when I could. It really felt like I found God when I found you two, then." I said.

"I do sort of wish we could just be some sort of trimarried female throuple. But Zax frickin' proposed after I only suggested he marry me, and now I'm stuck with my choice. It's a strange world." Dina said.

"I kind of feel the same way, us be a throuple. But then I had Jake cuddling with me whenever he could, and I kinda just went with him so he wouldn't feel left out from us three, even though Jake and I are two car-rion birds of a feather. And then Lucius pops back in, with his beautiful color, music, flowers, and love... It was impossible to say no to that. I do wonder how you and Zax started off your romance. When I was with him in your dream thing, it was nice, probably a once in a lifetime ex-perience, but it was rather unrealistic, since he looks *way* too much like Paul for me." I said.

"Huh. I'm a little jealous of you. You've found many ways to say 'I love you' to many different people." Dina said.

"It's the key to the heart, and there's not only one heart, or only one key. There are many loves in life. I just don't understand how you could give up on life for Hell." I said.

"I was going to take life, and love, and all else. I don't know. I guess I need some perspective." Dina said.

"So how do I get to Heaven? I thought only angels get to Heaven and I'm not an angel anymore- Oh." I said.

Heaven's pearly gates swung before me, and I waved to my old friend, St. Peter.

"Welcome back, Yule. We've been waiting for you." St. Peter said, and smiled nicely.

"...But..." I said.

"Our Father would like to speak with you, you don't have to stay if you don't like. Please, at least come to the garden with me." St. Peter said.

Dina trembled as she followed me, me going through a place I haven't seen in forever, so familiar to me.

I walked through the comfortable streets, the angels flying around and waving to us.

I heard familiar voices from a heavenly house. Felix said, "Nevaeh! Don't you think these tulips are... too colorful?"

"Nah, Felix. Just put them on the mantle, and let them bloom for eternity." Nevaeh said.

Maximus said, "You guys want to play some more football? It's the perfect weather out."

Fate said, "Oh! Yes, dear. I love watching you tackle. Although Max sure has been getting good at the game, so watch out!"

Max said, "Heck yeah, I'll play! I just got off work, and I'm feeling so energized and ready for fun!"

I wanted to not to be caught up in this bliss that tempted me. I was still alive... wasn't I?

Dina held my hand, and dragged me with her as I was about to charge in and talk to my friends.

St. Peter waved to God sitting in a lawn chair, and St. Peter went back to the gates. Dina gasped, trembled, and I bowed to God.

He invited us to sit on two lawn chairs beside him.

We sat with him, and God said, "Welcome home, Yule."

"Hi, God. I'm so confused, and I want to stay here forever... but that is not the right choice... is it?" I said.

God shrugged, and offered us both a beer.

Dina said, "I-I w-want t-to declare war- Peace? I don't know. You don't *seem* like you are this evil mastermind I pictured."

God started a joint, and passed it to Dina. She took it and inhaled immediately.

"Remember to practice temperance, my children." God said.

"Ah, whatever. You're always the first one to the party and the last one to leave." I said.

God grinned, and said to Dina, "I would prefer if you didn't upset my realm with your vast knowledge, Dina. I would still like everyone to be able to live in peace if they can."

Dina said, "But not everyone lives in peace."

God said, "Like I said, I would like it if they can."

Dina blushed, and said, "...So you mean I can't use my power in the living world?"

God winked, and said, "If that's how you want to put it."

Dina said, "I see... I don't want to disrupt your realm, but I want your promise to not disrupt mine."

I said, "Why do you want Hell, Dina?"

Dina said, "I want to build an even better Heaven out of the scraps of Hell. I don't care if sinners go there. I'll make them work, I'll give them family and community, and we will be happy. Happy enough."

God said, "That sounds like a good plan, Dina."

Dina said, "...Ok. So I have your blessings and your word not to intrude on my realm as well?"

"You always had my blessings, child. I will allow you to build whatever you desire. And Yule, thanks for guarding my throne as my seraph. I think you're doing a fantastic job." God said.

I blushed, and said, "I'm really a seraph now?"

God said, "Well, I was planning on giving you that job when you felt you were ready for it. I think you've been ready for a long time, Yule, and someone else already beat me to the punch in giving you six wings of fire."

I said, "But don't I need to protect your throne always and be ever vigilant? Don't I need to stay here, then?"

"Where do you think I'm sitting right now? You are guarding my throne." God said.

"...Oh." I said.

God laughed, and said, "Well, there are many other big chairs, small chairs, comfortable chairs or not, to sit on, but my favorite seat is that of creation. I wish for you to protect it always, until you come here again."

"...Ok, God. I'll come back one day, after doing all I can on Earth." I said.

God said, "Thank you, Yule." and we got up from sitting.

Dina was going to give God a well intentioned handshake, and God pulled her into a hug instead. Dina started crying, and said, "I really needed that hug."

I hugged God too, and we waved him goodbye, going back to life.

I felt sad as the gates shut behind me.

St. Peter said, "You know what to do, Yule."

"Yep, just jump off that one cloud. See ya, St. Peter." I said, waved to him, picked up Dina, and jumped off the cloud back to Earth.

81

Lux

"So is he a cat, or isn't he?" a child asked me.

I looked at Rasputin licking his butt, and I said, "Um... I'm not sure, kids. We've had a great discussion on metaphysical theory, evolution, and electrical sources, but I think we can take a break and watch TV for a while."

The kids all sighed out, and I brought out the rabbit in the TV.

Clippers turned on, said, "Hiya! I am Clippers. I am a TV, I guess."

The kids all oohed as the TV showed many old outdated sources of media, and I sat back and watched the show with the kids.

Clippers jumped out of the TV however, and began sniffing at the air. I said, "What are you doing, Clippers?"

"I smell... I smell... internet." Clippers said.

"I didn't know internet has a smell." I said.

"I- I- I need to help people. I need to help them traverse the internet." Clippers said.

"You'd rather not be a TV?" I asked.

"Maybe? I need to learn. I need more info... I must go. I am sorry." Clippers said.

"But... Who has the internet now?" I said.

"The internet is not the electricity and software. The internet is the connections of people. You are all the internet. I will go back into the ether, and be one with the net." Clippers said.

He hopped through a child, and then another, and another, and they chased the bunny and laughed.

Clippers looked happy, jumped at me as I tried to stop him...

But he passed through me, and I felt an amazing feeling of connection with life, the universe, and others. I felt what he was talking about, and it was the internet in connection.

He kept racing around, jumped through every child, and divided into more rabbits that jumped through more things, plants, an actual rabbit that was watching us, and Clippers continued to connect the world.

I sat back, and looked at the TV, that was only a blank TV now. Not even any power source to fuel it. The only power somehow came from Clippers.

"Huh. How did that work?" I said.

The cat was quiet, and let me wonder.

I tucked the children into bed, and bid them goodnight. I then recharged myself from the van's power source, my baby, and we slept together again.

I decided I would build the best school to keep people connected, to help them learn of life and the past. I woke up in the morning, stretched, and went outside to see Yule flap down with Dina in her arms.

Zax was smoking a cigarette and waiting up for them, and Lucius had just come back with a doe over his shoulders to feed the kids.

I cooked the feast with all the herbs he had as well, some roots and berries too, and used the last bit of the ramen packets to season it to perfection.

We were getting low on supplies however, and Yule and Lucius hugged me goodbye, we hugged Dina and Zax goodbye, and I went back to the school as the others left on their own life, a couple driving down the road in the van, and the other poofing back down to Hell.

I sighed. I felt kind of sad, strangely enough. I suppose just a loss for the life we all shared together.

But my life was beginning, as these young lives were learning. I taught the first lesson, starting with what my band called Tidings of Tulips did to survive and live, so the kids would get a little backstory of my own life and past, of the briefest moment. If I wanted to go even further, I would have to save that for another lesson or hundred lessons.

82

Jake

"I always felt like sort of the oddball out, Cass." I said, as we drank the beer in our pack on the porch, watching the horses make more horses after we found the mare a mate.

"I don't think so. I always thought you were nice. Even if you weren't because you drank too much." Cass said.

"I... I'm a little disappointed I couldn't have kept that relationship with Yule. I don't even want to think of her strangling me again anymore, but I do wish we could've worked past it." I said, taking a sip.

"I wish I could've fucked you all together in an orgy." Cass said, and sipped.

"...I love your dirty mind, Cass. The only one you missed out on was Lucius." I said.

"I know! It makes me the most frustrated of all! I was *this* close! But the dude had fucking relationships stuck in his head, over my hot bod!" Cass said.

"Eh. Maybe he's just a prude." I said.

"I don't think so. I'd always catch Yule and him sneaking off to fuck whenever they could. Maybe there's something about having that single, exclusive relationship I was missing." Cass said.

"...You don't want to get married, do you?" I said.

"Are you proposing?" Cass said beside me.

"God no. Let's never speak of it again. It's not that I don't think that would be nice with you, it's just... we'd have to invite everyone to the ceremony, our friends, our friends of friends, all eagerly awaiting us just to kiss and then wonder how we fuck each other as we consummate our marriage. Seems like way too much of a hassle." I said.

Cass giggled, held my hand, and said, "I love you, Jake."

I squeezed her hand, even though she couldn't feel it, and said, "I love you too, Cass."

We watched as the stallion just put a baby in the mare.

"You ever think we'll be like them? Have kids?" Cass said.

"Not if I keep using protection. I thought about it, after seeing those poor scared kids... and I never want to put another through anything like they had to deal with." I said.

"I don't know. We could try, one day? Maybe?" Cass said.

"Maybe. But let's try to make sure we have a nice life first, before we go and bring some kid into ours. We've got all those other kids to deal with now too, to feed and shit." I said.

"Oooh. Don't you think that darling Samantha is just cute as a button? I want to take her under my wing and teach her how to beat up anyone who messes with her." Cass said.

I said, "...I'm sure Lux has things handled. I hope we can find some other people to help us here, cuz y'know. Farming ain't a two people job. I got dreams, babe, and we're gonna have the best ranch in the world."

"I love when we can dream together like this." Cass said.

"Say... I forgot... What about Lux? I didn't even think of you and him- Did you?" I said.

"Nah. He's like my dad, in a way. Family is sacred, Jake." Cass said.

"...I guess he is a Pops to us. I never thought o' tha'. He's a good guy." I said.

"Well! I'm going to work on giving those horses some shoes!" Cass said.

"Horseshoes, right?" I said.

"I was thinking something pretty and pink." Cass said.

"...I think... I mean, I don't know, but let's check out that workshop out back. Aren't horseshoes supposed to be metal?" I said, as we got up and walked out to the back.

"Pretty metal! Just like my limbs! Cool. I can't wait to have a cyborg horse." Cass said.

I tripped on something as we looked at the forge, and I picked it up.

"Must be a lucky sign! Let's put it on the horse." Cass said.

"Ok. Yeah, this is probably a horseshoe. Yeah." I said.

We found the other shoes for horses, and went to figure out how to put them on the horses.

83

Dina

I had been anticipating this moment. But it seemed Satan did not want to show up to try and reclaim his Hell. I dragged all the demons back to Hell, in ways I sure you don't want to know about, whether they wished it or not, but Satan still evaded me.

Oh well. I got back home from work as Queen of Hell, I cooked dinner, Zax and I had a romantic evening, and if it was possible he'd have put another baby in my belly in our bed in Hell.

We had a rather nice house, a perfect little place. I honestly didn't care when Satan would show up-

But Satan slammed open my door, sweating, as Zax looked over my shoulder.

"I'm sick of this, Dina. Give me back my Hell." Satan said.

"I am sick of you. I'd send you far away… let you drift for eternity in nowhere… but I think it would be better… if people had a good long look at you." I said.

"…What?" Satan said.

"I think you're a rather interesting villain. A little too clichely evil in some areas, but you have no endgame agenda besides torturing us, and taking over creation, and yadayada. It's rather pathetic. But maybe *some-one* will like to read your story..." I said.

"Um. No... I think we can work things out! Need a gardener?" Satan said.

"No, Satan. I need a story to read, because I'm always looking for a new book." I said.

I looked at Satan, blinked, and looked again.

Satan was a book, a screaming story of evil, a burning book engulfed in fire.

I picked up this book as it screamed at me, and I shut the book, to let it sleep for another person's curious eyes. It was the end of Satan's story for now... and it was the end of ours.

And you also decided to close a different book.